Zawadi

& other short stories

Edited by P.Comley

Ouen Press

Published in Great Britain in 2020
by Ouen Press

Suite One, Ingles Manor, Castle Hill Avenue
Folkestone, Kent, UK
www.ouenpress.com

ISBN: 978-1-9996121-5-3

A CIP catalogue record of this book is available from the British Library.

Cover Design: Ouen Press, Main illustration: istock/Oleksandr Shchus

With thanks to
everyone who helped
make this project happen.

CONTENTS

FOREWORD

Once again we have been delighted with the response, almost overwhelmed by the volume, but always honoured to receive entries for this competition from all over the world.

Since the closing date for submission, the global pandemic and the measures taken by various governments and institutions to reduce the impact of the Coronavirus have affected almost every person on the planet. Existing injustices and inequalities have been exacerbated; there has been much sacrifice, loss and grief. It can feel at times like our lives have been shattered into fragments that will never be put back together.

While we may have all been somehow altered by our experiences over the past few months, some great thinkers of our time and in the past have highlighted these periods of great upheaval as opportunities, not to seek to go back to the way it was, but to respond to the situation with a renewed effort to build something positive out of the transformed way of things.

Many people have remarked that they have witnessed and experienced a wondrous generosity and a renewed acknowledgement of the need and value of community. Far from being broken into pieces, and beyond repair, as with a mosaic, the fragments of our lives can be reassembled, arranged differently to allow for a fresh view – an alternative, interesting and attractive way forward.

Although it may feel that somehow the stories submitted to the competition speak of a world before everything changed, we believe the themes are enduring and have much to offer especially in these uncertain times. The brief for the competition was a work of fiction involving a 'Gift' of any type, at any time or any place in this world or another. In this collection we learn about precious things that are embodied in people, places, ideas, talents, the joy in giving and receiving, the despair in losing, and the solace in recognising the value of what we have rather than wasting time, arguably the most precious gift of all, in anguish over what we have not.

Enjoy!

THE PRIZE WINNERS

S.M. CONNELL

S M Connell has written all her life, until now she has avoided the truth: she wanted to be a published fiction author.

At fifty-one, she is both writing every day and sharing her stories. Her first novel is in re-writes – *The Dark Conceit* tells a story we all recognise, one she's seen play out everywhere from Bourne End in Buckinghamshire to Bunkie, Louisiana: Sometimes the human power play for social domination is blood sport.

As a child she travelled. The first time she lived anywhere longer than two years was as an English major at U.C. Berkeley. Long before cell phones or the internet, she attended fifteen schools in five countries on three continents. Sometimes she could even speak the language, although everywhere but Khartoum, Sudan, provided reasonably safe drinking water and reliable electricity. During all these years there was only constant in her life, the written word, books she read and re-read, letters that took weeks to arrive, stories and plays she wrote but never shared. At eleven, she penned a book called *Why?*

Reaching adulthood she qualified as an attorney. Then quit law practice to marry the love of her life and become a stay-at-home mother to two kids who know where they're from, a sunny suburb in Southern California. Along the way, She's had two books of non-fiction published, *Acing Your First Year of Law School* (Hein & Co. 1999, 2nd ed. 2008), and *Get to Know Your Kid* (Stewart, Tabori & Chang 2011).

WINNER
OUEN PRESS
SHORT STORY COMPETITION 2019

ZAWADI
by S.M. Connell

Her husband waved away Nelson's offer of a second ladle from the silver soup tureen. With a curt bow, Nelson retreated to the kitchen, where Gift finished butchering a side of impala, sliced the loin into neat fillets, and set them to grill on the wood fire.

'When he's twelve, he'll start at Patch,' her husband continued. Raising his white wine glass heartily, he toasted the Patch motto, 'To the uttermost!'

Limply raising her glass, she beamed a facetious smile. 'Divide and rule!' she agreed.

His face darkened. 'Stop being ridiculous,' he grunted. 'That was always the plan.'

He was right, of course. It was always the plan to send Daniel Fletcher's sons to the Prince of Wales School in Nairobi. But the plan, when hatched, had also included a houseful of children, one of which was sure to be a girl, who wouldn't need to go away to school in Nairobi, who would stay at home in Mweiga and accompany her mother to the station on Friday afternoons to meet the boys' train. Moreover, said plan never anticipated her other children, those her husband knew only as an idea, or a briefly swollen belly. He never actually met them, the babies who flowed through the world in a river of crimson, smaller than a whisper, the babies Gift cradled and bathed and swaddled in muslin while Nelson dug another hole under the Baobab tree. As Gift murmured blessings in Kikuyu, it was she who lay her children to rest, bodies forever facing home. It was Nelson who blanketed the newly turned earth with crowns of violets.

Her husband also missed the arrival of the only live baby, having taken out the prop-plane for his Sunday afternoon patrol of the surrounding farms and grasslands. It was Gift who delivered the howling boy and placed the syrupy newborn on his mother's chest. It was Nelson who fiercely swept wolf spiders from the nursery and secured glass jars under the cradle legs to outwit the scorpions. While Gift settled umbilicate and afterbirth, stitched and comforted, Nelson set the sheets to boil, mopped and scoured blood from the floorboards, and her husband returned to find his son soundly asleep in his baby bed, bathed, fed, and trussed in a blanket. After naming the boy Daniel, Daniel celebrated new fatherhood with a good cigar and better whiskey, which Nelson poured from the decanter into a short glass.

Daniel scowled at his wife, fishing drearily in the vichyssoise with her soup spoon. 'Soup cold, Julia?' he inquired.

A sphinx's smile accompanied the spoon's release, heavy silver crashing to china. 'Chilled perfectly,' she replied.

At her husband's nod, Nelson's white-gloved hands cleared the soup plates. Once confident the houseboy was out of earshot, Daniel grumbled, 'He's only five. Are you planning to whine and moan for the next seven years?'

'That is my plan, yes,' she answered brightly. Cocking her head to one side as if a sudden thought tipped its balance, she asked, 'I wonder if you know his birthday.'

Muttering here we go under his breath, Daniel drank steadily.

'I'll give you a hint, shall I?' she continued. 'Danny will be six next month, and it's the end of March now. You'll just need to guess the date. Subtract six from 1953, and–''

He cut her off. 'His name is Daniel. And stop being absurd.'

Victory sparkled in the match flame Julia touched to her cigarette.

'I'm ridiculous and absurd because I dread sending our son away,' she exhaled. 'To a place you hated.'

'Everyone hates boarding school.' He finished his glass of cassis blanc. With a haughty sigh he added, 'Yet one must go.'

'Must one,' she parroted, her green eyes an oil slick of poison. 'And must he travel back and forth on his own? On the lunatic line?'

'Must I remind you who said the Kenya-Uganda Railway is the most courageous railway in the world?'

he asked. 'Churchill.'

After tilting his wine glass to confirm it was still empty, Daniel Fletcher drummed his fingers on the starched linen, impatient for Nelson's return. Julia smoked her cigarette to the filter, bashed it out in a cut crystal ashtray, and shoved the ice bucket toward her husband.

'For God's sake, pour your own bloody wine.'

He recoiled, blinking outrage like Morse Code, and resumed drumming his fingers.

With an ominous flicker in her venomous eyes, Julia taunted, 'And you wonder why the Mau Mau are coming for us.'

Daniel pounded a fist on the table. Shuddering china and silver were no match for the spectacular tumble of his red wine glass, an explosive shattering of crystal sending shards like diamonds skittering across the walnut floor. Instantly, Gift appeared to sweep silently, Nelson served plates of impala loin and roasted new potatoes then waited stoically, gloved hands clasped behind his back, for the Bordeaux in a fresh glass to be judged satisfactory. Once his servants disappeared, her husband said murderously, 'How dare you.'

Julia erupted in laughter. 'It's too good!' she howled. 'East African Standard: "Our man in Kenya has temper tantrum after soup course, incredulous that Mau Mau continue to fight back. One casualty, Baccarat. Africans clean up mess – no news there – but stay tuned for blood in the streets!"'

His grey eyes were a pair of blisters ready to spew cataracts of hate. 'We will annihilate the beastly savages by summer,' he vowed.

Her laughter abruptly ceased, taking her breath with it. 'Beastly savages,' she echoed.

'Subhuman,' he snarled.

'Yet it's immanently human to stash people in tin shacks without plumbing, pay them next to nothing, and rechristen them as a folly.' Feeling suddenly sick, Julia pushed the plate of bloody meat away. 'Admiral Nelson,' she scoffed. 'His name is Matu. Gift's name is Zawadi.'

'Gift,' he repeated.

'Poor old thing,' she consoled, 'Swahili's beyond you.'

'But not you, darling.' With his glass of Bordeaux, he toasted his wife, 'Here's to the middle class.'

'I've never pretended to be anything but the most middling of classes. African farmer's daughter. Unlike you lot, stealing Kikuyu land to live a life you could never afford at home. Bravo. Shall I raise a glass to you?'

'Take it up with my friend Sir Evelyn Baring,' Daniel bristled.

'I'm sure you two have loads to talk about. He's a baron,' Julia simpered. 'Your father was a greengrocer. From Wales.'

'We do, as it happens. Such as last week's events.' He paused for dramatic effect. 'When Mau Mau rounded up an entire village and burnt them alive.'

Julia covered her mouth, dramatically dropping her jaw in astonishment, then released the pose and casually lit a cigarette. 'Divide and rule,' she exhaled, shaking her head.

'Your ignorance is a bit depressing,' her husband observed.

'All of Kikuyuland knew about Lari the next day,' she snapped. 'And Naivasha. And the Home Guard massacre.'

'Massacre? They're terrorists!'

'You fool,' she sighed. 'We're the terrorists.' Julia slid her chair from the table and mounted the stairs, quietly closing the door to the guest room adjacent to Danny's behind her, never to return to the marital bed.

The sleeping arrangement but another element in an ever-growing segregation of the household. Weekdays from eight to eight and throughout weekends, Danny was Daniel, Julia was Madam, and Nelson the "houseboy". Gift administered bottles of powdered baby formula and the baby slept in his cradle in the nursery. When the toddler acquired speech, Daniel spoke only English, called his father "Sir" and shook his hand before bed.

In the off hours, Daniel was Danny, the baby Julia nursed at her breast, who slept in his mother's arms, and bathed with her in the clawfoot tub. Zawadi and Matu addressed Julia as Lia, her childhood nickname. Danny was Mwanangu, their beloved grandchild. They lunched on the veranda, Zawadi claiming the hammock, Matu the steps, Lia the chaise. Danny sidled up to his favorite of the day, cuddling against Matu's wiry frame, wallowing in Zawadi's ample lap, or resting his blond head on his mother's shoulder. The boy chattered in Swahili, Kamba, and Kikuyu, prowling behind Matu through the savanna tracking hunters and prey, learning birdcalls, and reading the stars. In the kitchen, Danny built fires in the iron stove with Zawadi, sorted beans and stirred pap, listened to her stories of the ancestors, the magic and mystery of the earth and sky. With his mother, Danny swayed in the hammock while she read him an endless parade of books, from Defoe to Kipling, Enid Blyton to Dickens. They sprawled on the kilim rug playing tin soldiers, built forts with bedsheets under the mahogany dining table, chased peacocks, and climbed flame trees. By the time he was ten, he could beat her at chess, and by eleven he was a better shot, both with a bow and a rifle.

In the evenings at eight sharp, headlamps announced the head of household's return, a pair of yellow eyes on the drive like a stalking predator, cueing Matu to stir a pitcher of martinis as Zawadi tucked Danny to bed with whispered tales of Kikuyu shape-shifters and kings. Lia kissed her son goodnight, dressed for supper, and like the rest of the cast, assumed her role in the evening deception. Elegant wife Julia, sleeping child Daniel, docile servants Gift and Nelson. Showtimes were reliable. The Administrator of the Central Province wasn't one to miss a day at headquarters or take a holiday. The cast never discussed the punctual duality of their lives; they understood it inherently, like two sides of a coin, or edges of the blade. Over the years, Daniel perfected his performance. Conversant in small talk, his table manners flawless, he was also an obedient co-pilot, politely enduring his father's Sunday exaltations of the Prince of Wales School, a subject his mother refused to discuss.

Lying on their backs under the Baobab one Monday afternoon, Danny and his mother tried unsuccessfully to count the fritillaries in the violets.

'What's the collective noun for butterflies?' she wondered aloud.

'A kaleidoscope,' he answered triumphantly. Spying a peacock in the bamboo grove he asked, 'Peacocks?'

His mother groaned, 'Don't tell me.' She squinted at the bird pounding his magnificent tail, preparing to raise his fan. 'Ostentation!' she shouted, and Danny clapped. 'Crows?' she asked.

'Too easy,' he dismissed. 'A murder.'

Suddenly, a frenzied clap of wings announced a mass exodus of weavers exploding from the west-facing branches, their red bills flashing like crimson shooting stars in a turquoise sky. Discovering the coast clear, the weavers returned in a cluster to the Baobab as quickly as they left, settling into its branches to continue crafting their intricate nests.

'How old was I?' Danny asked. 'When you taught me the world's always listening?'

'Three or four,' she guessed. 'Same age I was when Matu taught me.'

Danny thought a moment. 'We flew over Nakuru yesterday.'

'Too early for flamingos, I suppose.'

'I made a wish, and there they were. Thousands of them, like a lake filled with strawberry trifle,' Danny marvelled. 'A flamboyance of flamingos.'

'Lucky!' his mother cried. She took his hand. 'Good on you, Danny.'

'So I made another wish.' He rolled his head to the side, considering his mother's profile, her smile from ear to ear. 'About Patch.' Her smile disappeared.

She shut her eyes tight, like a child trying to wish away a monster. The habituated dread clutched her heart, wringing the bloody organ inside her chest cavity, a dread that followed her like a shadow, dread that she hid away deep in the caverns inside her and never allowed her son to see. Like awaiting an execution, every day was both the greatest gift and one step closer to the end. Her throat felt strangled, but she blinked her eyes open and managed a smile. 'Did it come true?'

'Yes,' he nodded. His face looked older all of a sudden, a passing glimmer of the man he might be one day. 'Seems he's gone off the idea.'

His mother stared. 'You're meant to start autumn term,' she said, wincing at the pain in her chest as she said the words aloud. 'In three months.'

'He said everything was spoiled. He kept saying everything was spoiled and ruined. Over,' Danny shrugged, eyes wide. 'Something about the Old School Committee being replaced, the government coming in. A new name, Nairobi School, I think he said.'

His mother sat up, leaned against the Baobab trunk, and peered at the peaks of Mount Kenya through the clear afternoon. 'They've lost,' she said. 'And they finally know it.'

Danny remembered another detail. 'He said they're going to ingest. Interim. Inte–'

'Integrate. It means Asians and Africans and Indians will go to school with the whites.'

'That's spoiled and ruined?' Danny asked, his bright blue eyes confused.

'Not to me,' his mother replied. As she lay back in the soft folds of the violets, the vice released its torturous grip on her heart and air filled her lungs, her ribs spread wide. Her body felt buoyed by the earth, like the tiny hands of her lost children were cradling her aloft. Overhead, the branches of the Baobab extended miraculously, reaching ever up and out in unabashed optimism, asking the sky with hope and humility for more, for better.

Danny smiled, his freckles disappearing into the dark suntan on his cheeks. He pushed a brilliant blond lock of hair out of his eyes and set off running for the house, calling to Zawadi, asking in Swahili if he could help with supper. Julia watched him disappear into the kitchen as the bird-chorus began, a symphony of weavers and doves, swifts, bustards, barbets, and nightjars. In the distance, a lone hyena called its mocking laughter.

She paid attention to the earth's remark. She'd spent a dozen years in fear and dread, counting the days until her son's departure, only to discover it would never happen. He wouldn't go to Patch. Another hysteric cackle echoed across the veldt. Julia pictured the skulking hyena, back haunches lowered in shame and self-pity. Matu approached with a heavy step, his work shirt dark with sweat. He dropped to a seat, leaning against the Baobab trunk.

'I'm a hyena,' she said.

'We are all hyena, sometimes,' he replied.

Julia offered him a cigarette and patted his work boot, admiring the new fence behind the bamboo grove. 'Looks strong.'

'Not to elephants,' Matu chuckled, closing his eyes, listening. 'Simba,' he whispered. 'You hear them?'

'Not like you,' she admitted. 'But good to have a fence when lions are about.'

They smoked, watching last crescent of sun

disappear on the horizon. A new wave of sound arrived with the dusk, singing crickets and frogs, the first eagle owl.

Lia frowned, 'Monday.'

Matu nodded, hoisted himself up, and offered a hand to Lia. 'Madam,' he said grandly.

'Showtime,' she replied, clasping his strong, weathered hand. As they headed toward the house, Lia linked her arm in the crook of his elbow.

By the time she emerged from her bath, Gift had whisked away Madam's khaki trousers, linen blouse, and dusty socks to the bubbling cauldron of laundry. Julia zipped herself into a crisply pressed floral dress, the attire her husband imagined she wore all day every day, not just weekends, and clasped a double strand of pearls at her neck. She carried a pair of modestly heeled white courts to the sitting room, where she accepted Nelson's generous martini pour. At the sound of the Land Rover, she wedged her feet into the shoes.

Lately, she and her husband spoke less and drank more, which combined to produce an analgesic effect on their marriage. Provided Julia followed the nightly procedure – cocktails, wine, first course, wine, second course, wine, coffee and nightcap – and strictly avoided any mention of the situation, she could politely retire after supper with her book, leaving Nelson to refill her husband's post-supper whiskey glass and replace crystal ashtrays until the master of the house staggered to his empty bed.

Tonight's silence, however, was different. Instead of smoking furiously, pacing and mulling over their next move, Daniel smoked as if the exertion of bringing cigarette to mouth was debilitating. He emptied his martini like swallowing medicine, and poured a second without Nelson's assistance. The white flag of defeat.

It was finished. Or as her husband saw it, spoiled. Armed by makeshift rifles with dummy magazines, machetes, spears, and arrows, the Mau Mau not only refused to surrender, they both held and steadily gained their ground, despite a colossal retaliation by (Daniel's friend) Sir Evelyn: A state of emergency that stretched to nearly a decade. Bombings by the Royal Air Force. The British Army, Kenya Regiment, and Home Guard on the ground. A million people imprisoned in detention and concentration camps. Murder and massacre, torture and dismemberment, castration with pliers, and rape with anything handy, from a Kenya Police officer dropping his Bermuda shorts to a broken bottle.

'I'm not feeling well,' Julia announced. 'I think I'll head up.' Her husband made no protest.

It was nearly eight by the time his son joined him at breakfast that Sunday, and Daniel received him with a customary glare of disapproval. As his son carefully removed the cap of his egg, Daniel Fletcher announced they would investigate Mount Kenya in the afternoon. Danny elected not to challenge his father's misinformation concerning the dormant volcano, nor did he supply the name of the third peak, which much to his father's frustration, eluded his memory. Bastion, Danny did not say. They were gone before his mother awoke.

Matu spent the morning back at the fence, repairing last night's breech. There was nothing to be had inside the perimeter of the Fletcher property that couldn't be found outside the fence, and Julia surmised the elephants trampled in protest, rebelling against the fence's absurd declaration of exclusion. They ate lunch outside, where Julia scanned the translucent blue sky, shielding her eyes from the noon sun, not wanting to miss the flyover. Matu returned to the fence, Zawadi to the kitchen, and Julia sat under the Baobab. A storm gathered to the east, a menacing hover of ghosts electrified by intermittent lightning flares as it crept slowly in her direction, dragging with it a low roar. Finally, the prop-plane appeared in the distance, both coming from and heading in the wrong direction. Julia leapt to her feet, waving both arms in the air to Danny.

In her print dress and pearls, Julia sat on the front steps chain-smoking, waiting for the glow of headlamps on the drive. Supper time came and went. After Gift and Nelson packed away the uneaten meal, Matu placed a blanket over Julia's shoulders and they bookended her on the step, waiting in silence as the midnight became tomorrow. In the night's darkest hour behind the bamboo grove, a crush of wooden planks landed in the dirt, the ground shaking from the thunderous stamp of massive feet. With a celebratory trumpet, they were gone. Julia offered Matu one of the last cigarettes from her packet.

The first cape doves called to welcome the orange glow of sunrise. Zawadi brought mugs of milky coffee and the box of cigarettes from the living room. She delivered bread and cheese for lunch, which went untouched. In the late afternoon, Julia stood for the first time on unreliable legs, drew the blanket closer to her body, and headed inside. She returned with a bottle of gin. Another night approached with a jumble of conversations, first the birds, then crickets and frogs, owls and animals. Matu turned his ear to listen to the contact calls of nearby lions, but the mechanic growl of an approaching vehicle brought the trio to their feet. A narrow pair of headlights crawled toward the house. Julia's bookends retreated to stand a deferential distance away as two officers exited the Kenya Police vehicle in unison, like schoolboys in their uniforms of short pants and knee socks. They removed their jauntily tipped caps and assumed appropriately grave expressions. Debris from a prop-plane had been found scattered on two rock outcrops at the point of impact, the base of Bastion. They were able to piece together the tail number, but the aircraft was completely destroyed. Because of the storm, animals reached the crash site long before the authorities. There were no human remains.

Julia's senses, all five of them, left her. Her brain ceased all function as her body released a wellspring of anguish. Doubled over and crouched in the dirt, shaking, vomiting, and dripping sweat, screaming, weeping, rocking. Zawadi squeezed her husband's hand as they stood watch, bearing witness to life's ultimate agony. At dawn, Julia crawled to the Baobab, bowed her wretched head against its trunk, and ripped out her hair one handful at a time.

When the sun set, Matu carried her to the house and placed her in Danny's bed. She buried her face in his pillow, inhaling her son, howling like a snared animal. She heard his hushed sigh, his intrepid laugh; she touched his velvet cheek, felt his kiss on her forehead. Grinding fingers into her scalp, she willed the pain to eat her alive, to end it for good, to set her free. With her fingernails, she ripped at her skin. Zawadi never left her bedside.

Days later, they stood together at Danny's window, watching Matu nail a simple wooden box and dig a final grave. As the flaming sun sank into the horizon, he covered the empty coffin with earth. By candlelight, he planted violets.

Julia returned to Danny's bed, refusing Zawadi's offers of food, a bath, anything. All she wanted, Julia pleaded in a hoarse whisper, was for them to move inside, to take a room in the house. Any room. 'Please,' she begged, 'Come inside. Like it used to be, when I was young. Before my husband.'

They granted her request, choosing the quarters off the kitchen. Together they tended their patient, managing to force into her sufficient fluids to keep her alive and sometimes the occasional bite of food. The violets bloomed and summer became autumn, but time had lost its meaning. Sleep, wake, night, day, light, dark, yes, and no melded together in a mad alchemy, one she would never again understand.

The only tether she felt holding her to earth were the lions. Females had decided to stay, settling near the house, patrolling and scent marking the surrounding territory each morning and huddling to sleep at night bolstered against the outer fence. One was pregnant.

In daylight from Danny's window she watched, and at night from Danny's bed, she listened. Seeing, listening, and hearing the earth, the bush, a fever dream, a cloudland. The cool mist surging through the savanna, blanketing the land in billowy fog. The Baobab. The bird-chorus in full, astonishing bloom, birthed by the ring-necked dove's rhythmic murmur, a terza rima. Time knotted into itself like the colours of the sky, memories melding with dreams, life with death, ends with beginnings. A cape owl with devil's horns alighting on the tendril branch of the Baobab. A skulking jackal, head bent low. The effortless glide of a white egret. All from her boy's window, window outliving boy. Over the evensong of birdcall and crickets, Julia shuddered at the unmistakable call of a male lion thundering through the dusk. After no reply, he roared again, a threat chilling and imminent, the sound of all sounds. His formidable roar echoed across miles, barbaric and raw, like a throat ripped apart.

Out of the tall grass a lioness appeared, her step weary, ribs protruding from an empty belly, four cubs in tow. Beside Matu's heap of wooden boards for his continual fence repair, she collapsed on a side flank, hungry cubs nipping at her dry teats. She kicked away the gnawing mouths, but they returned again and again, wiggling under her stomach, desperate for a mouthful of food, as the male roared his demands from a distance. For this mother, rest was an indulgence beyond her dreams. Tonight like every night, she faced her impossible task, the duty to provide forever undone.

With a guttural groan, she heaved herself upright and stashed her charges one by one deep in the safety of the wood pile. She circled her secret crèche, assessing its shield, and paused at the trampled fence. She looked up, through Danny's window, where her gaze met Julia's, a silent exchange of the unsayable truth: no mother has the power to protect her young.

We may fight to the death, but the fight is empty and futile and rigged from the start.

The lioness set her massive shoulders and turned her fine head away. As she headed out, her stride electrified, each step stronger, lighter, and more powerful than the last. Spine taut and resolute, muscles rippling under her golden coat, the valiant huntress disappeared into the night.

For the first time since the accident, Julia left Danny's room. Barefoot, she padded downstairs to her husband's office and opened the safe. On his desk, she placed the deed to the property and banded stacks of currency. On her husband's stationery, she wrote in capital letters:

> LAST WILL AND TESTAMENT OF
> DANIEL AND JULIA FLETCHER.
> WE LEAVE OUR WORLDLY GOODS TO
> MATU AND ZAWADI MAINA (NELSON
> AND GIFT FLETCHER).

She signed her name, forged her husband's, and dated the letter with Danny's birthday, April 22, 1947. From her left hand, she slipped off three gold rings, her wedding ring and those of her parents, and placed them in a row under Danny's birthday.

Their bedroom door was closed but for a crack, the house dark and secured for the night. Julia dropped her cotton nightdress to the floor and stepped outside, shutting the door quietly behind her. In the moonlight, the naked mother knelt under the Baobab tree, brought her forehead to the violets, and said a last goodbye. The red earth reached through her skin, demanding she understand. Her children were there. They were the earth, as was she. She was the red earth on which she took her first steps and Danny took his, that cocooned her lost children, that welcomed her now, that welcomed Danny. All earth, all one in the same.

Overhead, the sky was a million stars. After resting a hand on the Baobab trunk, she set off across the yard, wove through the bamboo grove, and tiptoed across the gap in the fence. With a jubilant heart, she crouched beside the wood pile. Slowly, the hidden cubs peeked out, greeting her with their soft sounds, a lullaby. On the red earth, she lay on her side in a crescent, welcoming the luxurious fur on her skin, the caress of young paws, four heads nuzzling against her warm belly. Embracing the tiny royalty, she curled herself around her infant warriors and slept a night of bliss sublime.

At dawn, the lioness headed back to her children, exhausted and empty-handed, as the hungry male's roar angered across the savanna. Julia woke to a low, purring growl. Huge, wet nostrils sniffed at her smiling mouth as whiskers tickled her chin. The mothers locked eyes, amber and green, for the second and final time.

T. H. KUNZE

T. H. Kunze is a Scottish novelist and short fiction writer. After graduating from Edinburgh Napier University, sojourns in America, Asia and on the Continent all shaped the compelling sense of perspective that kick-started his author career. A writing course with Curtis Brown Creative and frequent contributions to literary forums helped inking the nibs.

Successes to date include short story publication at Hammond House, various international competition placements, and an unflagging resolve to keep creating against the odds.

When not revising his promising third novel or grooming a growing short story collection, TH can sometimes be glimpsed shredding guitars like his hopelessly imaginary alter ego. He calls it research.

RUNNER-UP
OUEN PRESS
SHORT STORY COMPETITION 2019

WALKING ON AIR

by T.H. Kunze

It takes me around ninety minutes to restring an acoustic guitar. Others might do it in under ten. Or maybe never.

Unwinding the old strings sets in motion an irreversible process, each haunting glissando a shuddering moan from the instrument's heart as life-giving tension drains from its arteries, turn by turn. Best practice demands slackening strings in a mirror sequence, from the outside in, to minimise neck distortion induced by the briefly imbalanced tensile load that substantially exceeds my own bodyweight.

Once released from the self-locking bite of its tapered bridge pin, a twitching, dissonant rattle of dead metal spells the end of each string's vibrant, single-minded existence, celebrated by the billion-or-more tuneful oscillations I've extracted over the course of its life in rapt self-abandon. A life remembered as so much more than just another dull piece of wire on the carpet, even when my clenching fingers twist and coil the six-strong tangle into a sturdy loop, ready for disposal before the real work begins.

If you've never felt the desolate ache of a disembowelled guitar, imagine one morning finding your computer's keyboard reduced to a solid plank of plastic. Or a car without wheels, a snow globe without snow... You get the idea: despite its physical sensuality and elegance, an unstrung guitar is emotionally immobilised and – to my humble musician's eyes at least – ostensibly naked. Maybe that's why it becomes such a joy to clean.

Relieved of its six-bar prison, the matte ebony fretboard always seems wider than before, and featureless besides its obvious partitions at logarithmically diminishing intervals and the notional order imposed by seven small, circular mother-of-pearl inlays. Closer inspection reveals the faint haze of wood grain, scuffed and mildly worn in places along the second, fifth and seventh fret: clear evidence of my fingers' favourite dance spots, corroborated by minute dips in the adjacent metal fret pieces. Neither will significantly impair playability. Instead they form part of an organically evolving imprint; a unique identifier, the pass code to my musical soul, and an irrefutable reminder that no one gets to play this guitar but me...

'Allison! You going to be much longer?'

Phoebe: my flatmate, keyboardist, and devil's doorbell. She will soon be wearing a ripped-black steampunk mini dress with studded waist, and Vegan

Chrome 1460 DM ankle boots. For now, the deployed hood of her gothic moon-phase sweater and pale zombie-gauze leggings tell me she's raring to hit SoundLand.

'Told you, I'm restringing before we–'

'You haven't even changed out of that manky tracksuit yet!'

My duster continues to work its way up the ebony track, methodically, before descending on the delightfully accessible headstock.

'I'll be another hour, at least.'

'Jings, Allie...' Her kohl-blasted eyes flare with a glint of angry silver.

But not for long. She knows I dislike being called that. Not that either of us has ever brought it up since, but we had sex once. More of a productive fumble, really, catalysed by her then newly acquired lacquered corset she had asked me to lace up. I waited until afterwards to politely inform her that I stopped being an Allie at age twelve. Even when sweetly whispered. Both Al or Allison are fine.

'Alright,' Phoebe sighs contritely. 'I'll go by myself, then. Just wanted you to see it before I... You know?'

'Look... How about I take a break after cleaning? Gives the polish time to soak in, so I can string up when we get back?'

Phoebe's smile blossoms like a black tulip, sends her into a cross-legged floor sit to face the sofa bed where I've laid out my stall. Reaching for a fresh cloth I can sense her inky gaze tracing my every move, restlessness smothered by studied curiosity, while I address Sitka spruce and sapele with the caressing care of a post-natal advisor. A sharp sniff from below when the scent of lemon oil cuts the air; just a single squirt from a tiny bottle before I work the rich yellow liquid into the fretboard to remove surface grime and revive its natural obsidian glow.

'Right – that'll do it for now.'

Even a coiled spring wouldn't do her justice.

o0o

Edinburgh buses can feel like the horticultural equivalent to icebreakers. More than once a low-hanging branch smacks against our roof as we tunnel beneath Queensferry Road's park-side canopy, and I can't help wondering if we, and not the City Council, are its officially assigned tree surgeons.

No-one else up here seems to notice. Two girls behind us – probably in their mid-teens, but I don't turn to check, obviously – now debate the pros and cons of rival chocolate spreads with a decidedly liquid lilt to their echolocation voices. Both will soon be wearing fuzzy fleece zip-up pullovers in cool mint (my left) and toffee brown (my right), and identical skinny-stretch tortured denims. Phoebe on the aisle seat beside me has at last descended into a pre-acquisition torpor, remains tongue-tied even when a handsome if hawk-nosed man of around our age slinks into the front seat opposite, soon to own a recurve archery longbow with superior stopping power capabilities. I'm not sure how that makes me feel.

We get off at George IV Bridge and saunter down Victoria Street to the Grassmarket. It's a sunny spring day and thus rammed with experience-hungry tourists questing for duck-lipped selfies. SoundLand looms invitingly beyond, a haven of creative sanity and sudden magnet to Phoebe's gel-cushioned pixelburst trainers, their teeth-shattering four-day delivery delay forgotten at last. I can barely keep up with her, deflect the titanium-tipped sting of pain with thumping steps, until she looks back, stops.

'Sorry!' A grave nod at my right leg. 'Implants playing up?'

'Nah. Just wonky paving. Let's go.'

Once through the double doors, quietness returns. My kind of quiet: a vast, cubist, wraparound horizon of freeze-dried expressive potential, suffused with the distant licks, blips, beats and squeaks that politely waft in from all sides, heard but not seen. Phoebe beelines it to the synth section tucked away at the ground floor's far end, behind a defensive phalanx of respectable home keyboards, Rhodes rip-offs and the odd upright piano.

'So, that's the Monodactyl,' she welcomes me back, stabs out a volley of howling notes on its stunted keys before mangling the fading sound wash with indiscriminate knob twists.

'OK... Shreds it.'

'I know, right? And this...' a bubbly skip to the next rack, 'is the MicroBurst.'

Another cascade of old-school robotic grunts, harshly melodic, coaxed into oblivion by a series of pitchbend rolls, in perfect sync with Phoebe's ecstatic eyeballs.

'Good growl,' I say, and mean it.

Only, I don't really. We both know that her keyboard needs are comprehensively covered already by a Nord Stage and a Mininova synth. The former is the lipstick-red mandatory monster to legitimise any band's performing credentials, incredibly versatile, and a mighty graduation gift from Phoebe's recently US-domiciled parents. The latter kick-started her keyboard career, kebab-shop funded while still in art college three years ago, and even sports a Kraftwerk-style vocoder with swan-neck microphone.

'So you're after that analogue vibe?'

The milk-faced assistant appears from nowhere, hovers barely beyond arm's reach behind us, and will soon be served his comeuppance.

'Yea, yea, I'm kind of hooked,' goes Phoebe, on the turn.

He eyes her up, clearly approves. 'I've the Pterodactyl, myself. This one's big brother. Yeukie wee beastie, I don't mind telling you.' A sly glance at me. 'You both in a band?'

'Aye,' Phoebe says. 'Sisters Of Cacophony. She's the guitar, me the keys. Our drummer's probably still in bed.'

'Pure wallop name, that,' he commends her, then wags a fluffy chin at the rack. 'This pup will help race you to the next level.'

'How, exactly?'

His glaikit stare hits me just milliseconds before Phoebe's. 'Well, it's analogue...'

'Yeah?'

'So, you've got, like, the return of true seventies classic warmth–'

'Reverse-engineered, to run as an emulation on a modern digital chip, right?'

'And that wooden back panel...' He taps a grainy-brown strip the size of a large ruler bearing the company's name. 'That's a killer stage look.'

'You mean, real wood? Or killer plastic?'

'Uh... Let me find the manual, OK?'

Phoebe's longing gaze follows him, then slams into me. 'What did you have to do that for? He's being helpful. And kind of cute.'

'He's a salesman.'

'So? Let him sell me the good stuff.'

I find my mental windscreen, wait for the next wiper swipe. 'Guys like him sell style. Not quality. So unless you like pissing away your money...'

'Down a wooden latrine, no less,' she grins, tugs at a spike of raven-black hair.

'Mock-wood, probably.'

A furtive glance. 'Ok. Let's bolt, before he finds out. Tough titty, kiddie – I'll buy online.'

o0o

Light as lint and commercially unburdened, we drift with the GPS-enabled tumbleweeds until a cafe-shaped wormhole yawns open, spews us into orbit around an Italian supernova. Two elegantly dressed couples perform their table evac manoeuvre in a loud but leisurely fashion, spatially and socially oblivious, until a heated debate followed by the grudging click of a one pound tip seals their withdrawal's fate. Both ladies will soon be wearing turtleneck tartan tunics that cover body deficiencies and highlight the charm. Probably after their ghoulish tour of the Blair Street Underground Vaults.

So, I have TMM: transient metacrystalline memory. Less by way of affliction, I think, than the serendipitous discovery of a dormant mental faculty. Just a sniff of text, the glimpse of an image or a shred of speech, and their raw imprints remain etched to the inside of my bubble for around ten minutes. And I don't just mean as the hollow, dreamlike outlines of complex objects, akin to the hand stencils found in early cave art. My cerebral prisoners are fully formed, yet exist there as indeterminate data, like uncharted constellations or loose puzzle pieces, unless and until I choose to interrogate them. And with the shameless wealth of data now aired in public via our portable broadcasting centres, I'm often tempted.

The symptoms started after the accident, nearly two years ago when I still lived at my student digs in Merchiston. Last week's finals safely tucked under my zero-G belt and borne on the winds of infinity, my flying bicycle clipped a passing car, just beyond The Mound's steep S-bend descent. Even now I can't say whose fault it really was. And what's the point, anyway. What I do know is that our relative velocity vectors intersected unfavourably, and despite braking hard both of the car's left tyres crunched over my flailing right leg to the tune of a complex triple fracture. They reckon my helmet prevented the worst.

Once the red mist lifted and reality had rattled through its painfully slow reboot, all seemed as it should be: the sobering white-walled sin bin, splashed pink on either side by conditionally relieved parental faces. It was only after their departure, when my lids slammed shut with a leaden thud, that the new layer of consciousness began to wink at me in the dark. Elusive as stray light on clear glass, like outside glare from a TV screen, readily ignored when watching the bigger picture until – snap – focus shifts, irritation wins, and we shut the curtains. But my drapes were pulled already. Which made the surprising images in my head a lot harder to dismiss. Not least because of their near-holographic resolution: the rolled-toggle leather buttons on Mum's fraying cardigan, the maudlin inflections in her stoic voice, my dad's monogrammed signet ring and the tickertape football scores on his clasped mobile... Vivid, if arbitrary, mementos of our strained encounter, lined up on my mind's brand new browser interface, ready for detailed inspection, whereupon their content simply transferred itself to the more familiar regions of my memory. Those browser entries unopened thankfully faded from view after a few more minutes, until a tingling veil of quiescence descended at last; that portentous inner silence charged with the knowledge that something in my life had changed beyond the dull bite of twin callipers on splintered bones.

Obviously, I tried blaming it all on the drugs, at first. But no show. While their cocktail of antibiotics and painkillers diminished along the road to youthful recovery, my mind's fidelity upgrade clung firm, rewarded me with a bumper pack of sensory confetti during my very first crutch-wobble up and down the busy ward. Come release day, I was nervous. But needlessly – my newfound reality simply leapt past the hospital gates, perfectly in step, like a faithful pet.

I've since learned how to winnow its bountiful stream for life-affirming curiosities while discarding mere trivia on the self-recycling neuron heap. What at first threatened serious information overload has, by the very nature of its comprehensive choice and clarity, bestowed in me the new, quiet certitude of existential beauty; a strangely liberating rear window view on human perspective I'd rather not live without anymore. Though I still wonder sometimes if these enhanced perceptual powers simply mark my belated ascension to everyone else's level of normality? You tell me.

One thing is certain: I cannot assess whether my cognitive renaissance sprung to life at the expense of any previous social skills or intellectual abilities. For what it's worth, I'm known as polite and forthcoming at work, and have never yet forgotten my front door keys. But who knows what redundant circuitry lurks inside this skull of mine? Surely no conscious being, biological or otherwise, can investigate their own mental integrity beyond its inherent boundaries? Like the event horizon skirting an invisible black hole, the singularity of being is an unobservable absolute, as impervious to reason as reason itself, and hence no amount of yanking at our own hair will ever pull us from the quicksand of existence. Others may claim the ability to do so on our behalf. But their analysis is solely based on the visualisation of cause and effect; the ephemeral, spectre-like shadows we cast by the harsh point-source light of their leading questions, hastily traced in chalk and catalogued along with the DNA samples, like evidence at a crime scene. Maybe that's why I've never mentioned my little box of tricks to anyone.

'Single espresso, please,' I answer the feline-faced waitress, smug in my pre-emptive victory over her obligatory double entrapment. She nods curtly, and will soon take delivery of a Celtic Tree Of Life aromatherapy necklace to heal her chakra.

o0o

'How about we lose a beat? Turn the middle into seven-eighth?'

Phoebe frowns, stabs a keyboard button to stop its burbling arpeggio. 'You mean, seven beats to the bar? That's kind of freaky.'

'It adds tension, yea,' I explain confidently. 'Keeps the audience awake. It's our last song, remember? And it's called *Wauchle* – nothing says "stumbling with fatigue" like a dropped beat.'

Behind the drum kit, Doug shuffles restlessly. 'Not easy to dance to, though.'

'Depends on how you dance. And it only lasts for twelve bars, so...'

'I doubt there'll be much dancing, anyway.' Phoebe to the rescue. 'Half the crowd will be queuing for drinks.'

Doug looks strategically unconvinced, reinforced by the tufty shudder of his side-swept, sugar-brown pomp, on fleek throughout even the most explosive of drum fills, rare though they may be. In seven days he will be performing in acid-washed patchwork festival trousers and a wolversloth T-shirt. For now, his dripping skulls top is overdue at the laundrette.

'It's simple, look...' I strum him a choppy sequence of chords while counting out time, soon accompanied by a stomped tattoo from Phoebe's spinach-green 1460s, arrived yesterday.

'Alright, I got it,' says Doug, sticks twirling. 'Let's give it a go.'

But it doesn't go well. Bouncing steadily along an eight bar run-up, each time we cross the rhythmic Rubicon Doug's flailing arms begin to resemble a swimmer's first attempt at the butterfly. I try not to laugh as we wheeze through a few splashy laps before Doug breaststrokes ashore.

'Sorry,' he goes, panting. 'The groove's gone, I think.'

Phoebe and I nod in unison. 'No worries, Doug.' She turns to me with an edgy grin. 'And no more spanners, eh? I'm leaking enough oil as it is.'

In almost exactly one week's time the three of us are due to reach for the stars. Little wonder, perhaps, that both Phoebe and Doug have slithered into their spacesuits already, cocooned from risk contamination and focussed on nothing but the silver-thin trajectory of stellar injection burn.

Me? This may sound heartless, but I remain emotionally ambivalent about performing in front of an impatient crowd, half-cut and hell-bent on just one thing: to see the backs of us. I haven't told the others – and probably never will – but as truth stands, their astronaut antics increasingly remind me of actors in monkey suits. In my world we'd all be back in Doug's studio right now, laying down quality Celtic Prog House tracks for a proper shot at the identity-conscious local media, not flogging our EP's worth of couthy knock-offs to a few punters wasted beyond the point of care.

'I make that twenty-two minutes,' Phoebe reads off her phone's timer after our final run-through. 'I doubt they'll taser us off the stage for that?'

Doug gets up, shakes his head. 'Nah, two minutes over is fine.' He yanks open the stiff rehearsal room door, lights a roll-up to hydraulic squeals from a loading bay outside. 'At worst we'll catch a few hand signals from the manager.'

It's Doug who swung us the gig at Sneaky Pete's. His brother works there sometimes, and hence kindly helped bump us nearer the second front of a long line of unsigned bands hoping to cut their teeth at one of Edinburgh's best-renowned indie venues. We'll be opening for Loorie Lou, a somewhat more established four-piece from Bathgate we'd never heard of let alone met, promoting their new album of crust-punk gloom.

'What are you planning on wearing, Al?'

I deflect Phoebe's sneer at my default denims with hardboiled insouciance. 'My guitar, most likely. But honestly, I've not given it much thought.'

Shrouded in a lazy plume of smoke, Doug turns our way. 'Me neither.'

Liar.

o0o

To some, the contour plot before me might resemble a strangely psychedelic Landranger map of mountainous terrain. However, traversing its vast blue lowlands to scale an isolated red peak, the uninitiated eye would soon struggle to link this apparent topography with the depicted underlying geometry. You'd have to strap on your geek wings to spot that the colours here don't signify shape at all, but dynamic performance. Data which, once resolved, can punch home the near unbearable thrill of predicting when your medium-sized delivery van might career over a cliff edge.

'That's the modified brake calliper?' my passing boss enquires.

I nod, pinkie-point at a lurid feature on my screen. 'Three mil larger fillet radius here, and the higher grade SG iron. Looks like it'll pass their rig tests this time.'

'Good. Can you run me some fatigue life shots, please? I'm due down there tomorrow.'

'Aye, no bother.'

Half-turned, he pauses. 'Fancy coming along?'

'To Manchester?' I peer up at him. 'We've a dress rehearsal that evening, for–'

'Oh, your big breakthrough gig. Day after tomorrow, is it?'

'Uh-huh.'

'In that case – don't worry, I've got it covered. And Allison: best of luck!'

He walks off with the sympathetic smile of an aspiring part-time poet inured to publisher rejections. Which he is. His outfit tomorrow will include a customer-proof navy-blue suit with threadbare cuffs and one of his three gold-chequered ties. By Monday he'll be back to pleated black trousers and casual white shirts.

'Thanks!'

He isn't the only reason why I like working here. This unassuming design consultancy on a drab little industrial estate near Turnhouse airport hired me when I still moved by means of tri-pedal propulsion, and even fixed a handy retention clip for my crutch to one of their break-room tables. Pinpoint solutions: too many people still seem afraid of that sharp, openly self-motivated strike at the heart of a problem, instead prefer hiding the audacity of their own flawed existence in the twilight of hopeful uncertainty. Before tripping over someone's walking aid left lying on the floor. With a laugh, of course.

My structural analyst job here might not appear as glamorous as that of a four-star hotel's catering manager, for instance. Phoebe, too, turns more heads on any day when mentioning her online fashion business – hand-printed cotton tops dyed in our iridescent bathtub when she's not working at charity shops. And Doug, well... His gap year now approaches its third solar orbit, fuelled by the cosmic guilt of a divorced father. But glamour or not, we're all of us tilting at the windmills of our lives, one sail at a time. Mine just happen to be visible.

Something makes me swing by the orthopaedic shop on my way home. I have to wear a two-centimetre heel lift on my right foot to compensate for pulverised bone – at least when conducting "strenuous exercise" which, evidence pending, I reckon could include stage performance. Both my existing pairs of surgical shoes are black, perfectly normal in outward appearance, and very comfortable. Yet here I am, browsing their meagre shelves on the off-chance of hitting it lucky, until the assistant who knows me by sight conjures a blood-orange twosome of Rebounds from her storeroom.

'Snazzy!'

'Returned this morning,' she grins. 'Wrong heel wedge. But just about right for you, I'd say. Try them on.'

I do. Once standing up I can't help striking a power chord pose, hypnotised by the sanguine vitality now claiming the floor beneath me.

'Comfy wee devils, aren't they?'

Even my smile must be walking on air. 'Yamba! Just the lift I needed.'

oOo

I'm a machine... I'm a machine...

My silent devotion to this meditative emergency mantra is not lost on Phoebe and Doug as they squashball from wall to wall. Not that the gloomy brickwork of our dressing room would even fit a ping-pong table. But right now, no one seems to mind.

I'm a machine. Designed, built, tested and calibrated to play music. Being observed while doing so will *not* impair my functionality, because the laws of quantum physics do not apply at Sneaky Pete's. Hence my program will execute flawlessly...

'You alright, Al?' my patchwork-trousered drummer wants to know.

'Uh-huh. Just running through the set list to–'

Our door opens to the sound of a single knock.

'Five minutes, alright?' One of the stage-hands, his round face beaded with sweat.

Behind him, two of Loorie Lou's band pace the corridor nervously. Seeing us they make a point of offering a shifty wave.

'Dancing,' one of them grunts for our benefit.

I'm not. Our so-called soundcheck has lasted all of two minutes, forcing me to rush the cabling-up of my vital guitar effects panel. I now find myself spooling back through surprisingly hazy mental records for potential wiring faults, when Doug stops in mid-bounce to address us.

'I'm good for seven-eighth, by the by.'

'What?'

Grin rising, his hands waft out a rhythm.

'For *Wauchle*'s middle. I practised at home.'

'Thanks, but no thanks,' barks Phoebe. 'Next time we play the Usher Hall, maybe.'

I'm about to weigh in when the call comes.

The next five minutes smear out in weightless disbelief. Like a tribal ritual, my senses implode to frenzied howls from the barbarians below, a hundred or more chiselled shapeless by blazing stage lights, until somewhere, somehow, our opening song plays itself to a vaguely harmonious end, and lightly-toasted applause.

Halfway through our second, more upbeat track – and against all forecasts, contour plots and lances shattered – I'm beginning to enjoy the movie. It's still impossible to tell if the colour-strobed audience agrees, but frankly, I don't care. Until the song's emphatic final crescendo elicits a widespread salvo of whoops and air-punching fists.

I can't believe this.

And even less what happens next. Still lapping up ovations, I catch sight of the manager sprinting towards us from stage left.

'Can you stretch to thirty minutes?' he shouts as we huddle around the drum kit. 'Or thereabouts? Lou's still AWOL but we're trying to track her down.'

'No problem!' I hear myself reply to him and my golf ball-eyed band members.

'Great, thanks!' He slinks off with a sheepish thumbs-up at the mildly intrigued masses.

Phoebe's smile at me is strictly commercial. 'Heavy raging, Al! What are we going to do?'

'Improvise.'

And we do. With only two more rehearsed songs in hand and twenty long minutes to fill, my movie turns epic, tells of crusades and the fearless migration of a displaced nation, all to the haunting soundtrack of unchained climactic beauty. Borne aloft by the ever-rebounding power of blood-orange, I exhume traditional chord progressions long extinct from the Celtic gene pool, shocked to a life renewed by Phoebe's snarling bass lines and the pagan doom summoned with every beat of Doug's thunderous incantations. We're out of control, yes. But something tells me it's not just the crowd who like it.

Come *Wauchle* time, the answer is written all over the brave, copper-winged heart motif emblazoned on Phoebe's pretty steampunk dress. I suddenly wish I'd made more of a fashion effort myself, to celebrate this moment, to sublimate my humdrum standards of civility to the soaring spirit of legend. And the edge on Phoebe's dreamy look at me seems to agree, if only politely, before we both turn to find Doug's steely grin firmly underpinned by seven raised fingers. Two intrepid nods, and we're away.

Perhaps it's this audience, now at full capacity, their magnetic push and pull palpable and synchronised to our rhythm... But when we trade glances, when the beat breaks, it's like a strained cord snapping, the final barrier unhinged and discarded, and a room transformed by the jittery ecstasy of unresolved bliss. And not just out there – the seventh wave pounds my own chest, too, over and over as I riff on each rolling swell, soon swept far out to sea where gold-skinned demons rush in to keep my titanium-packed body afloat. Just in time to catch a glimpse of Lou, smiling graciously from the sidelines beside one relieved manager, and for our freefall to regular altitudes.

Closing chord belted and now hooked to my plumped canopy of applause, the swaying floor approaching beneath me seems more permeable by the second; a fractal sponge, each hole the gateway to its next porous microcosm, and the next...

I'm unsure when exactly I touch ground. If ever.

o0o

'That's fifty!' Phoebe proudly proclaims, one day on.

On the sofa beside her, my neck cranes for a better look at the tiny graphic – sales statistics from Bandstand, online home to our fledgling EP offering.

'Pretty decent for half an hour's work. Downloaded albums, or single tracks?'

'Mixed,' she says. 'But still–'

'Look at these comments...' I snatch her tablet, home in. 'This guy: "To these ears, you kids nicked the show from a proper loused Lou last night. What's your excuse?" Wow, this needs a reply!'

Phoebe smiles lazily, curls around her refilled cup while I read on, buoyed by the warm, ceaseless current of shared kindness, repaid by my tapped-out approvals and absolutions; all common currency, self-minted yet legitimate, and aching to tip the invisible scales of happiness.

Even as I write, a new sale registers, startles Phoebe with its coin-clatter sound alert.

'Feuch – tasty top, that,' she nods at the profile photo provided by our latest supporter.

'Too right it is!'

I stare down my future's hawk-eyed guardian, then hit Search, and will soon be wearing a pink leopard's leap cold-shoulder blouse with gloss sequins to express my individuality and uniqueness.

JONATHAN SHER

Born in 1993 and raised in Givataim, a city at the centre of Israel, Jonathan was the last addition to a family of two parents, two daughters, and 4 cats. He grew up loving books (especially those that featured animals), dancing, and watching Cartoon Network. Spent his preteens and early teens acting in several plays at the most prominent theatre houses in Israel, enjoyed making up stories since elementary school, and studied cinema at the Thelma Yellin High School for the Arts.

During his mandatory military service Jonathan served as a military journalist and editor of the IDF ground forces Facebook page and website. After his honorable discharge from the military, Jonathan spent the summer as a martial arts guide at Camp Ramah in California, stayed on to tour the U.S and then on to Mexico.

Back in Israel, Jonathan enrolled at the Hebrew University of Jerusalem, taking their Interdisciplinary Honors Program in the Humanities. Jonathan spent the last semester of his bachelor's degree as an exchange student at Sciences Po – The Paris Institute of Political Studies, receiving the European Erasmus+ scholarship for exceptional students, and received his B.A. at the end of 2019.

RUNNER-UP
OUEN PRESS
SHORT STORY COMPETITION 2019

REMOVED

by Jonathan Sher

I am a memory. Most of all, a memory of a boy on an operating table. The burn of alcohol-infused throw up choking my throat, colouring my breath. Keep drinking, they say. I should be blacked out. I should be entirely numb. I am neither. I feel the fingers of the men separating my flesh. I feel the knives grinding through my bones. I do not hear a thing. I might have been screaming and crying. But that is not part of the memory.

There is no comfort. What I am most desperate for are the eyes. Like water. They started changing the moment I got sick. As always, it could be seen before it was felt, and soon it was confirmed by those men with the knives that are used for men. My parents look sad, embarrassed, angry. At who? I know it is me they are angry at, even if they don't say it. No one was ill in the previous generation, on either side. It was unusual. It was phenomenal. They were beginning to feel safe. And now here I am. I am making them do this to me. I am making them remember – anyone can get sick.

There is no comfort. As soon as it starts my dad goes white under his trimmed beard. He went to the barber early this morning to make himself more presentable. Did he believe he was doing it for my sake? When we embrace, before it begins, he feels stiff and cold under his suit.

'It's going to be all right,' he coughs in my ear.

His hard stubble scratches my cheek and I put my hand to it to check if there's blood. Boiling water. Soon he disappears, but not mom. She is brave. Her lips clenched tight in effort, her dark brown eyes hold on to me for a long time, desperately, feverishly hold on to me, growing bigger, growing horrified and red. Now they are gone. Her face is turned to the side. But still, my hand. Her hand. Her fingers wrapped around mine. Not warm, but solid. Slowly they open. She allows my arm to drop down and away. I want to reach up to her, I want to see her face again. Am I calling to her? Is my voice reaching her ears?

You must remember your sins if you want to be free of them. I am in the old cathedral, bathing in the orange and the purple sunlight flowing through the coloured glass. Nature touches me through the work of man while I cry. My brother pushed me down and now I'm hitting my sister and running away, hiding behind the big oak confessional. Hollow sounds vibrate the stone columns, clenched tightly by the still, mouldy air. They are coming from the great organ up there on the wall, angels and chimeras climbing its sides, mixing fangs and hooves and solemn faces. Not exactly a tune. One sound slowly climbing on top of the other and then going down again. The organ is dying, I think. Then I remember it's nothing but metal and wood. Was this when it happened?

I wake up in a husk of foreign flesh. It has been removed from me, or I from it, and now I'm trapped inside of it like a spider in an overturned bowl of glass. This body is lying on a white bed, tucked beneath tight sheets. Without looking out the window I know I'm already away. I'm already in that place. Time passes. I stay still. What used to be a man walks into the room, every part of his body covered by an orange gown and a matching veiled hat that covers his face. What remains visible under the veil makes me scream. My new voice flows like sewage, covering me from the inside out. The man's dead eyes show nothing. I force this body I'm in to turn away from him. It makes me dizzy and sick, and exposes the right arm from under the sheet. It is rotten even though it is intact. I realise that I am the same as him. I throw up.

It is the first time I see a non-person. I am running on my way to the butcher to get mom bones for the casserole. The opening to the market street is blocked off by people, but I manage to squeeze through the coarse winter skirts of the women. Now I see her, the non-woman carrying herself like a burden, seemingly motionless as she slowly drifts along the shops. She reminds me of the poisoned cat we killed with rocks. I don't know why we did it. At the end he just sat down, bloody, one eye smashed and leaking, looking at us. Cursing our souls. Is this when it happened?

I remember the terror mixed with excitement when for a moment she is looking at me. Through me. She is looking for something, something that was taken from her. Maybe this is what did it. Maybe that's all it takes. Something covers my eyes and I sink down layers of fabric.

'No need for you to go scaring the boy like that. Walk away now,' my self-appointed guardian calls out.

I stay motionless for a while. Could be ten seconds, could be ten minutes. When I shake myself free I run back home without looking back. I am breathless and sweaty. We do not have bones in the casserole and everyone is upset with me. I tell them nothing. I relish my secret, my right for indignation. It is before they sent them, sent us, all away.

I am in the white bed, unmoving, careful not to expose any part of this body that is sobbing non-stop. Irritating little motions, ugly sounds, yet I can not make it stop. I don't eat, I don't drink, even though the orange man comes in and replaces the trays and pitchers on the table three times a day. It keeps on going. The first time I realise this, I almost suffocate. The horror. It keeps on going, never turning back. That was the moment of choice – follow on, or get out. Most children choose the latter. They cry and cry and after a while they are silent and after a while more their breathing stops. Neither choice is valiant. But a choice is made. I start to feed this body that disgusts me. To water it. I do not choose death.

It is evening time. A candle lights the typewriter on my desk. I am here and I am not here. I am never now. It is an unwinnable race. Always one step behind, what I see, what I feel, is the past. The only question is how far back I am carried away. And perhaps another – if it is not me there, in the moment, who is it then? What sort of creature guides my feet to its sunken tracks? But that is not important to me right now. What is important is that another chapter has been set to paper. Deirdre is reunited with her lover, but is not as joyful as she had anticipated. She is beginning to doubt her initial judgment of his character. Was she being childish as her sister claimed? Beginning to doubt also her own decent nature. She has lustful thoughts, ones that can not be dismissed as misplaced longings now that Aldus is no longer away. A grey gloved hand plucks the paper out from the machine's soft metal grip and places it at the top of this evening's pile. This machine has given me dozens of lives to experience, to play with. Deirdre's, as most, does not hold the promise for much pleasure. I rise from the chair and carry the candle across the moaning floorboards. The flickering images of a bedroom take shape around me. The heavy blankets are uncomfortably warm, but the extra weight, taking a semblance of chains for this body, soothes me. The gloved hand places the candle on a chest next to an open envelope. It grabs the note from inside the envelope and spreads it flat in front of me. I did not write these words.

A meeting is requested with the mayor. Who is this mayor? I think to myself. What does he want? Time passes. Yes. Tomorrow after the work in the fields is done, I will go. I blow on the candle and it blows back darkness. I turn back to the now invisible note. I believe the words I saw etched on it remain the same, though why, I do not remember.

The chariot is waiting for me as was written. There is still plenty of light, but we create our own shadows using cloaks and veiled hats. He is a purple shadow. He does not turn his head to me but does not turn it away either. Courtesy. I can just make out his profile even though I keep looking straight ahead. Disgusting. I wish I could get a better look at the horses, but I can't. We do not speak as it is not necessary.

We stop in the city, in front of a normal two-storey building. I was expecting something grander. I was being silly. Who is there to impress? I get out and wait until the sound of the chariot rattling away disappears completely. How horrible it must be to live in the crowd, I think to myself again. How lucky was I to be placed in field work. I walk up the stairs and drop the brass knocker twice. It has the shape of a hare. Soft steps are heard from within and the door opens.

Crimson garments. Freshly washed. I raise my head. The veils are not nearly enough at this distance, leaving the face blurry but tangible. White skin, blue eyes. Soft and unthreatening jaw line. It hits me like a kick to the gut, but we are practiced, our expressions controlled and flat.

'Good evening,' he says with a surprisingly deep voice.

In the days before it would have probably been considered dignified. Now it has all the charm of a toxic swamp belch. I return the greeting with my equally terrible higher pitched version.

'Please come in.'

The drawing room is large and well kept. Heavy wooden furniture, a half dozen leather sofas, cabinets filled with books. Dim lighting seeps in from the outside, carefully regulated by thick velvet drapes. This is more what I was expecting. He turns to face me again as he reaches the far end of the room. Slowly, he brings his hand up to his hat and removes it. I do the same. Courtesy.

He is young. His sharp eyebrows and broad cheekbones make up for the lack of character in his chin. It is apparent that he shaved right before I got here. Why bother? I wonder. He wants to show me something. He was once beautiful to behold. Even now it is like looking at a skilled artist's depiction of a decaying corpse, that was suddenly brought to life. It's even worse than our normal wretchedness, like some kind of sick joke. And he wants me to acknowledge it.

'Well, now that the precarious part is over, let us sit,' he says. He is referring to the attraction – the reason why every encounter of our kind is a risk. Minimal, it's true, but still. We sit at the two most distant chairs. Courtesy has its limits.

'Can I offer you a drink?' he says and gestures at a crystal bottle half filled with ruby liquid. It emits a faint glow. Some of the older ones, who had a taste for alcohol before it was forced upon them during the procedure, still drink it here. Alone. Always alone.

'No, thank you,' I reply.

A crimson arm pours the liquid into a low wide glass, and circles it around the still air. It is not raised to his lips. 'Do you know why I asked you here today?'

'No'

'Would you care to guess?'

'Is this a test? Or a game? In any case I am not interested.'

His hand stops circling but the liquid continues to stir like a physical echo. His smile is an opening of a wound in his rancid meat of a face. We rarely smile.

I read some of your books. Are you playing the grumpy old man from the lighthouse now? What was his name?'

'Goodbye,' I say and stand up from my chair.

'Fine, we'll keep it brief. Please sit down, I promise you it is a matter of great importance.'

I sit.

'It does concern your books. You know they read them, you receive your royalties by mail. Not that money means anything to us here, and I assume they know that, but maybe they think it's only fair you get your share. What do you do with it? Hang it on the walls?'

I remain silent. He nods.

'But perhaps you are unaware of the number of readers you have. From what I understand, there's hardly anyone who doesn't read them. Are you surprised by your success? I would be. Personally, I find them utterly unimaginative. Childish fears dealt with grade school vocabulary, reaching predictable ends. Yet it's clear to me why *they* love them. Why they love you.'

He pauses, and suddenly his expression turns very grave. This has been rehearsed, I think to myself.

'It is exactly this predictability that matters to them. These books are a proof that you're human, that we're human. That we can love, and dream, and fuck even. Or at least that's what *they* seem to believe. A protest movement has been born and it's been gathering strength. They're suddenly asking themselves what life looks like in our city, and if perhaps there could be a better way. Coexistence, rehabilitation even. And now there's been an election. They've won. Their president wants to meet you, wants you to help them think of a plan, wants you to be the bridge between our worlds. What do you make of all this?'

He shoots this question at me like a dart. This really is a test, I think to myself.

'I…' I am off balance.

This is what he was aiming for from the start. Did he think I would lie to him? Why?

'I…'

I did not realise I still wanted this. Unthought, unthinkable for all these years. I am searching for my resentment, looking to find some steady ground, but it suddenly melts and reveals a soft, aching, forgotten stump of hope. I am thinking about my family.

'I… I think it might be a good idea.'

A sigh of disappointment. He sits back, for a moment looking away, resting himself from the sight of my face in order to arrange his thoughts. Then he empties his glass in one gulp, leans back forward, and fixes his eyes on me.

'What is it you think separates man from beast?'

'Oh boy'

'Please. I am only asking for you to hear me out. I believe that as the representative of all of us, it is your actions that will decide our fates. I will not, I cannot force you to do or say anything. All I can do is beg you to participate in this conversation.'

The intensity in his eyes seems to draw us sickeningly closer.

'I am willing to listen, but I will not participate in your rhetorical games.'

He nods.

'The only thing that separates man from beasts is religion. God is one of humanity's first creations and perhaps its deadliest one. This is perhaps common knowledge in our increasingly secular times, but what most people seem to forget is that religions don't revolve around a single all mighty and benevolent protagonist. No, as a writer you should know better than me that a story like that wouldn't sell. What brings the action to religion, what drives the plot so to speak, is the fact that next to the solemn God sitting calmly on his throne, stands the smiling devil.'

Crimson fingers swirl underneath a horrible face, slit from one side to the other. I notice how much dimmer the room has gotten. Soon candles will have to be lit for us to see anything of each other.

'Are you implying that you're the devil?'

That happens too. Some become delusional after the operation, but usually they don't last long afterwards.

'Not me, us!' He nearly shouts.

'Hardly anyone believes that anymore. You're arguing from two hundred years in the past.' I say wearily.

'Oh, but they do. They just don't say it, don't think it out loud. As the church grows weaker and the abstract devil loses faith, we grow more important, we become not only an image of the devil or his works, but the actual incarnation in the flesh.'

I am a boy on an operating table. The pain is unbearable yet it goes on and on and I feel it and still I am. I am the pain. My mom looks away from me. From what I am becoming. Her hand lets go of this sinful creature. Is that penance I see in the back of her head? Is she purified, redeemed, through my pain?

'All right. Let's say you're right. How does that work with this new movement you claim to have won an election? They want to help us, they might actually care.'

Contempt crawls like a handful of vermin across his face.

'They don't care, they don't remember! Decades have passed since the last of us walked their streets. Even family members aren't allowed in the operating room now. All they know is that one day they might get sick. What sick actually is, they can't imagine. Sure, they heard the stories, but they need to see it. This is not a generation of blind faith. They are conducting an empty ceremony, and that just doesn't cut it for them. But when they get what they are asking for, who knows? Best case they'll just bring you back here and put your voyeuristic literary career to rest, or at least until the next generation claims their right to see damnation face to face. But it could also be much worse. They could decide we're a horror too great to be permitted existence. Decide it's time for a holly purge, a crusade. And as you very well know, we devils are defenseless.'

Attraction makes it almost impossible for us to work closely together in large numbers. I am on my way to the shoemaker to pick up a new set of boots. I am not thinking about boots. I am thinking about a story, the first one I will ever write. It is cold and the wind ruffles through my cloak like a spiraling sheet of ice. Just as I pass a deep blue color, the wind lifts up its veil, not completely, but just enough for me to make out his face from the side of my eyes. There is no word for what I feel, but then again, there never is. It is a thirst that transcends physical dimensions. Perhaps lust is the term. I do not know because I have never felt lust, the operation came too soon for that. I do not find his face less disgusting than any of the others, yet it calls to me, or rather, to this body. It consumes it. I want it to stop so I move. Luckily, he is stronger than me. Luckily, others are there to hold my face to the ground while he runs away. They talked about this at the hospital, I remember when I am again able to think clearly. They said it is unpredictable but fixed. I must never see that man again. They said to turn and run the moment you feel it happen. They said people do terrible things, some eat the other's flesh. They told me no one is able to resist it the first time, so they hope I'm lucky. They said women and children, like me, are most at risk. Keep your face hidden. Look at no one unless you must. You will not be able to protect yourself. You will not be able to stop yourself.

I am sitting in a dark room, staring at a monster.

'What is it you think I should do then?' I ask. He seems to flicker in his hesitation.

'Don't go. Refuse the invitation.'

It is now my turn to force a smile, and I fumble for the muscle memory. Did he practice that too before I came? Mirrors are objects we use with caution.

'You only wish this invitation on yourself. If I refuse, it is you they'll naturally choose to deal with, mister mayor.'

This opportunity to see life, even for a moment, might never come to any of us ever again. He is now barely visible. A pale spot atop a faded redness.

'For the sole reason that I believe I will be better able to handle it. For the sake of all of us. But you don't believe me.'

I do not contest this.

'So I will only beg you to heed my warning – there will be no great changes for the best, there will be no redemption brought to us. Tread lightly. Do not get your hopes up, do not believe their promises, for you will be gravely disappointed when they take them away, and in your desperation you might do something rash, something that will doom us all.'

He is now unseparated from the darkness of the room. A tortured, bodiless voice.

'I will take your warning to heart,' I say. Courtesy.

'They will come for you tomorrow morning. If you change your mind…' He does not bother to finish his plea. Everything is dark now.

'Your carriage is waiting outside,' he says after a while.

I almost forgot he was there.

o0o

I am a boy on an operating table. I wake up because of the pain. I look for my faceless, distant mom, but even she is gone now. It is just me and the doctors. I look down. There are three of them hunched over my open chest. All wearing masks, their brows gleaming with sweat, their eyes as wide and unblinking as a sharks' closing in on its prey. Maybe that's lust. My body splits in two, and then again, and again, until it shatters entirely as the doctor between my legs pulls up a gooey ball of tar-like substance. It screams, like a baby might scream if it did not need to pause for breath. The doctor looks up at me, his face stretched in alarm and then in horror. I wake up drenched in sweat. Is it a dream or a memory? Is it or is it not who I am?

I am sitting in the horseless metal carriage that propels itself forward. It is not magic, the man said, but something called steam. It is still early morning and as I peer through the curtains I see the town waking up. Things have changed. Streets are wider, cleaner. Shops are more colourful, and have unbelievably vast glass windows presenting their commodities. There are street lamps all around, and they too have changed. They are brighter now, and too high up to be reached with the lighter. But all these changes I notice in passing, for what my eyes latch on to are the people. They are beautiful. The children, the old, I know that it is love, true love from first sight, that I feel for them all. Amazing. How could I forget the way people, real people, walk, stand, casually touch their hair, their face, each other even. So different from the coerced, tense way that we hold our bodies up, trying to keep each part of it as far as possible from anywhere else, as far as possible from itself. They are so carefree. Natural. My vision is blurry. I am angry at my lack of control. I want to see clearly. I want to see more.

I am in a small side-room of a grand building, the new town hall. There is only one small window that faces an inner courtyard, and it too is covered by rich satin drapes. Nevertheless, the room is well lit by bright humming glass candles propped up on the walls. I stand restless but motionless. I am being made to take off my garments for them to be searched. Being naked is unpleasant for us, and the man they sent to make sure I was not keeping anything from them, turns so green and pale I think that he is about to faint. Still, that is not the reason why I cannot take my eyes off him. It was he whose privacy is breached, not I. I am filled with love and compassion and guilt. I am ashamed. I am happy.

Now I am in my garments again. I am not in control, I think to myself. I cannot be this weak, I say to myself. A knock comes from the door.

'Yes?' I say. Even this sounds theatrical. Fake.

The door slides open and reveals a man. I remember him, yet he is here. I remember a face like this, looking at me from a bed across the room.

'Is it really you?' his voice is cracked. Already eyes watering up. He starts to pull his nose. I remember being jealous of him. Bigger, stronger, more liked by dad. I remember thinking he was less intelligent than I was. That I will be richer than him, than them, that I will be important, and then they'll see. I remember wanting him dead. Just for a little while, just when he'd hit me. I don't remember loving him. Why is it I feel love for him now? Maybe I am confused. I remember him well, yet here he is.

'Take off your hat, I want to see your face,' he says while shaking his head. 'Please let me see your face.'

I slowly remove the veiled hat from my head. He tries to control his expression, but he fails. He is not experienced. He is in pain. I see myself reflected in his face. I start raising my hat again, but he protests.

'I'm so sorry,' he says, looking away. 'I'm so sorry,' he says again and again, struggling to keep his eyes on me. After a while he manages to do that, and calms down his broken breaths

'I am not going to ask you how you've been, because I know it must have been horrible. It must still be horrible. But I want you to know how proud we are of you. How proud I am, of my little brother.' His voice catches again. 'You made us remember you. Not only you, but each one of you, each one that gets sick and is sent away like he's someone else's problem. Things have changed, we're modern now. We don't have to keep following the old ways, the old mistakes. There's talk about stopping the deportation, and hack, one of these days they might even find a cure! There must be some way, some hope for us to live together. I… I have a wife now. Two girls, eight and five years old. I want you to meet them. I want them to get to know you. Look…' he searches inside his front pocket for something. Even his embarrassed confusion is graceful, like some sort of dance. He walks forward, and reaches out a shaking hand. A grey hand takes the brownish cardboard rectangle and pulls it up.

'I'm sorry,' he says. I look. An old woman is sitting on the front porch of a family house, embracing two girls. Brown and white colours, too real-looking to be a drawing. I do not know this world anymore, I think. I do know her.

'Where is dad?' I ask. He shudders at the sound of my voice. His jaw drops.

'He got sick two years after you did. Didn't you know? I was sure someone would have let you know. You never see him over there?'

I look back at the woman and the girls. Teeth together, lips curled up and to the side.

'It wasn't easy, losing him. And of course you before that. I had to quit school, get a job. But I guess it worked out in the end. I have six stores now, sell dental equipment to all the big dentists out there. Where's that smile? That's what we're called. I'm no writer, but I came up with that name.'

I offer the cardboard back to him, but he shies away.

'No, no. You keep it. It's a gift. They're coming you know. Mom and my girls. And Martha and Henry too. They're all gonna be here out front in just a couple of hours. You'll get to see them in person, and they'll get to meet you, the famous author. My god, it's really going to happen. We're going to be one big happy family again.'

I am a boy on an operating table. I am being moulded by hot pain.

I – am sitting in front of a typewriter. Grey gloves tick away, but they are not important now. What is important is the boiling onion soup that the maid just spilled on General Blackbeard's groin while he was planning the pincer move for his surprise attack. Cursing and flailing at the crying woman he changes his mind and decides to head straight for his enemy's weak spot without pause. If it had happened a day earlier, he would have won the war.

Am – looking for mom. Why is she not with me in the hospital? Where is the boy who used to look at me from across the room?

A – hard rock is pushed into the side of my face. I am screaming. I want to get up and chase that man. I want to turn him into ash.

Boy – is he going to regret it. He's going to regret hitting me, laughing at me, yes he will. I'll wait. And then he won't see it coming. I have time.

On – the hard sun-stricken ground of the pumpkin patch looking up at the cloudless sky. The crows are clawing at the trees and calling my name.

An operating table – keeps me steady. Floating on a waveless sea. Why am I here?

I am sitting on a raised wooden platform in front of a crowd of hundreds, thousands of people. I've never seen so many people in my life. They're all huddled together, touching, they don't mind it at all. I wonder what they smell like. I sniff the air but all I can smell is the inside of the veil. I wish I could touch them. Not with these fingers, this body. For real. I am ashamed to stare at them directly, but I do it anyway.

To my right, a few feet away, stands a man at a podium, wearing a closely fitted grey suit. A lighter shade than my garments. Fashion has also changed. He's been talking for a while. Such a lovely voice. Words blending into each other gracefully, like drops in a lake, like the bodies in the crowd. I know I should be paying attention. It's not fair to ask that of me. I remember the mayor. I cringe at the memory of his face. How easy it is to forget. The crowd claps. In the front row I see children. They are not crying. They are not dead. They stare at me with interest. They sense I am somehow forbidden. For them I am a wrapped Christmas present. I am something new. The crowd is clapping again. I turn to the right and see the man's hand is stretched towards me.

'Get up,' someone whispers in my ear. I comply.

The clapping increases and washes over me. I am a rock on a beachhead. I am protected in my veil, I think to myself. They are protected in my veil, I think to myself.

'Come on. Go to the podium!' the voice says to me urgently.

I turn and see the suited man wave his hand fervently. I walk over, float over, carried through the air. Where have my feet gone to? I reach him. His eyes are tense over an overexerted smile. He reaches out his hand. I am confused.

'Go on. Shake it!' he exclaims loudly.

He masks it well, but there is a tension in his voice. A gloved grey hand reaches out. It is pulled up and down vigorously. The crowd roars again. Louder. I see them shouting, some crying, some laughing, some looking up, hands together in prayer. I remember what the mayor said. I see an old woman standing in the first line right in front of the podium. She is holding two girls tightly to her, one to each of her bosoms. This time she is not looking away from me. Repentant, almost begging. It is not me who is offered redemption, I say to myself. I am angry when he let's go of my hand. Instead of letting it drop I hold it up and to the side, the same way I used to in school. I could see through the teachers' smiles, through the thin coat of approval that covers the contempt one naturally feels towards anyone too eager to please them. I didn't need to read through my fellow students' expressions. At first he tries to ignore me, this is not what they told me to do. Not what I agreed to. He keeps waving to the crowd and starts walking away, but he looks back, and I keep my hand up. I am a good boy. This time I really can wait. Slowly, the most eager members of the crowd start hushing the rest of them. Finally, there is silence. They're all expecting it and he can no longer walk away. He looks worried, threatening, but he's still smiling as he comes back to the podium.

'Is there something you want to say?'

Courtesy. A grey gloved hand is lowered. Then it goes up, takes hold of the top of my hat, and pulls it up. Air is released from the crowd as it unanimously deflates. The man, eyes narrow, slowly walks backwards. The circus trick has gone wrong. There was something in the hat after all. I step in front of the podium and turn to the crowd. Claps, almost hysterical, first just a few spread far apart, then slowly gathering confidence and reaching the same excited level as before. I look at the old woman with hands on the two girl's eyes. She's looking straight at me, defiant, loathing. These are not the eyes I am looking for.

'Things have changed,' I say loudly. Another wavering of air from the crowd supplemented by screams from women and children. But again the claps come back, more quickly than before.

'This city has changed,' I continue, and receive cheers of encouragement.

'But things are not different.'

I pass my gaze on the silent crowd and feel it sink like quicksand under its weight.

'I am a reminder. There is no comfort. There will be no escape.'

I turn and run towards the suited man. He tries to run, while two others come towards me, but this body is quick. I jump and sit on top of him, and holding his head back I run the cardboard rectangle I received across his exposed throat. Then I am pushed to the ground.

'I'm fine, I'm fine,' I hear him say. 'Fucking monster.'

I do not resist the hands holding me down but I wish they would turn me towards the audience. I want to see her eyes again. I think about the mayor. He was right, I think to myself. I was a bad choice. I only remember myself.

Removed by Jonathan Sher

HIGHLY-COMMENDED

F.S. WILLIAMS

Sarah Williams lives in Krakow, Poland where she teaches English and French. She believes it is a country offering a wealth of literature, music, and history with a story waiting to be told in every city square, every monument, every castle, and every person you meet.

Sarah was born in Stratford-Upon-Avon, England: Shakespeare country, a promising start for any writer she says. But from the first year of her life the family moved and never stopped moving until she left for university, sometimes up to once or twice a year. While she admits this could be difficult, it gave her a chance to meet a plethora of people from all walks of life. She noticed how much she loved guessing the story behind each new face, each smile, each tear, and even each frown.

After university, she continued the nomadic lifestyle and lived in Tunisia, Spain, China but it was not until she moved to Russia that things began to change. Russia is a writer's dream with literary greats such as Dostoevsky, Tolstoy, and Bulgakov peeking out of every corner ready to provide influence. Moscow is a city that gets under the skin and alters a person from the inside out, she confides. She knew this when her writing took on a life of its own and she began to write full-length novels with characters she loved and hated in equal measure. There, she wrote her first novel about three women struggling to live a normal life during the Siege of Leningrad.

When not looking for new inspiration, Sarah says she loves reading, hiking, travelling, and trying her best to learn Polish, an adventure in itself!

HIGHLY-COMMENDED
OUEN PRESS
SHORT STORY COMPETITION 2019

THE VIOLIN OF BUENOS AIRES - ERNESTO

by F.S. WILLIAMS

Ernesto tottered into his study and dropped the violin onto the table. He sat down and unbuckled the case with shaking hands. Ignoring the heaviness in his limbs, he leant over the violin and looked at it closely. He would polish it first, that was easy enough, then he would fix the bridge back into its proper place. He supposed he had dropped the case on the boat coming to Buenos Aires or somebody must have bumped into him with a lot of force because the bridge tilted towards the neck at a precarious angle. Although he hadn't seen it for years, he knew it hadn't looked like that before.

He picked up the bottle of polish and his fingers trembled as he tried to unscrew it. Tiny darts of pain went up his hand. 'Come on,' he said, 'please.'

He set it down on the table and held onto the sides of the chair, waiting for the electric waves to stop flowing through his arms. A door slammed upstairs and somebody ran down the corridor in the flat above. Ernesto picked up the bottle and let it fall on the floor. The glass smashed into small, shiny pieces, the polish was thick, brown and spread out on the floor like treacle. Careful not to fall over, he leant to one side and dipped the cloth into the puddle. He began in circular motions, lightly in case the wood had gone soft.

'How did the dust get into the case?' he asked out loud. He wiped away the thick layer from the violin's neck and found another cloth in the drawer. If he had time later, he would give the case a quick polish as well but that only needed a floor cloth and some warm water. Some of the marks on the black leather may have got there on the boat. There were times when he left it in the cabin and he was sure someone had taken it out of the case once or twice. He wasn't sure if he should wipe off Liesek's name which he had written on the case. If Ernesto held it close, very close now that his eyesight was leaving him, he could just about make out the individual letters but from afar, it looked like a white splodge.

The fumes from the polish felt like a brick wall coming closer and closer to him and he put his hands on his chest to brace himself for the pain but now, it didn't come, only a strange, hollow sensation was in its place. He swung around and opened the window, the effort making the veins in his hand bulge and twitch.

The noise from the traffic outside crashed and whined so he put the radio on. Gardel's voice filled the room and Ernesto thanked God his son hadn't tuned it onto the American channel. He couldn't stand listening to the whining voices over an infernally loud beat. Ernesto sang along, singing stopped the swaying motion in his head so he sang with more concentration than he usually did. The words died in his mouth once when the blue cloth worked around the edge of the violin and he found the white marks. Thirty years before, Liesek had dropped it on the brick pathway leading up to Ernesto's house. 'Oh Jesus!' he yelled out and looked round in case anyone heard. They took it inside and played Mozart's Concerto No. 3 to make sure the strings weren't damaged.

'Serves you right for taking it out of the case outside anyway,' Ernesto told him.

It was Liesek's idea to try and serenade Heidel Volzke who lived down the road. Ernesto was to hide in the bushes and warn him in case her mother was coming up the road. Heidel's father had chased them away. Ernesto swallowed a bitter, hard lump in his throat and polished the neck careful not to grip it.

Heidel's father cheered loudly enough for the whole street to hear the day he and Liesek had to leave Liefenstrasse. When Ernesto caught his eye, he gave the Hitler salute. All the time, Liesek was looking up at the windows to see if Heidel would wave him goodbye.

Ernesto gripped the sides of the table and let out a few rasping breaths that cut holes in his chest. Without warning, Elvira walked in, her wide, solid figure filling out his vision. Her black hair was scraped back in a tight bun and he looked at the few stray hairs by her ears as she leant over the table. His tea. Everyone still laughed at the way he prepared it with a strainer *'just like they do in Europe'*. Elvira set the tray down and looked at him for a few moments.

He looked up to see what she wanted and was surprised to see her pointing at her upper lip.

'You've got something,' she said, 'just here.'

She handed him her handkerchief. He wiped his face and the blood looked bright red when he took it away.

'Thank you. I'll buy you another one,' he said and went back to polishing the violin, ignoring her hard stare that that stayed on him until she left the room.

After a few minutes, he stopped and looked at the violin properly. He had done well, the wood gleamed and reflected the window behind him. He lightly brushed the underside with his calloused fingers. People had always remarked on the unusual shade of wood, most dark wood violins looked black after a good polish but this one still retained the gleam and beauty of an old tree. He wiped his forehead trying not to touch his face with his polish-stained fingers. Gardel had stopped singing a while ago and two unfamiliar voices were discussing the new proposed State that the President had suggested a few weeks ago. Ernesto stood up, but an invisible weight pulled him back down on the chair with a loud thud. He pressed his hands to his eyes and waited for the forest of stars to subside. His front side felt almost gelatinous and he hauled himself back up until he was almost spread eagled on his chair.

The radio's tinny voice kept on and the words mingled in his head until he could only pick out individual phrases. *'Economic strategy, head of state, no finer act of patriotism.'* The two voices kept going and in his worst nightmare, he was spinning down into an abyss with only them for company. With flailing hands, he tried to turn off the plastic monster. With a surge of effort, he pushed himself onto the floor and crawled over to the cupboard to switch it off. For a few moments, he stayed where he was, cramped into an uncomfortable position on the floor, hands over his face and waiting for the sickly warmth in his body to cool down.

When he stood up, he tried not to notice his left leg shaking in his corduroy trousers. He sat back down at the table and looked at the violin as if he were looking at it for the first time. 'The bridge,' he said to himself and picked the small chisel, the size of his little finger, out of the blue, leather packet. A few more white marks wouldn't make much of a difference, but he was still careful not to chip off anymore of the varnish as he eased the bridge away from under the strings.

Putting a bridge in the right place was a two-minute job which he sometimes did for free if he was in an affable mood. Now, the bridge was trembling in his hands where pins and needles covered the skin and spread up his arms like boiling water. He held out his left hand and breathed hard several times. When he was ready, he flexed and curved his fingers until the feeling almost came back.

He kept most of the glue bottles in the cupboard but luckily, he also had one in the drawer. It wasn't the strongest type, but it would hold. With one hand on the violin's neck, he dabbed a few streaks of the bitter smelling glue and placed the bridge on top, hard enough for little clear bubbles to appear. With his heart in his stomach, he picked up the violin and held it up to the pale sunlight, holding his breath. The relief nearly pushed him over when he saw the perfect angle of the wood and it took him a few moments for him to get his breath back.

The next job was the strings. Now, he felt a little stronger and, although his legs were going numb, he could still shuffle over to the cabinet. For about ten minutes, he looked over the packets, lined up in neat rows before giving up and taking all of them back to the desk.

Liesek had put the last set of strings on himself, almost thirty years before. They were hanging around Herr Heldermann's workshop while he fixed a broken peg on Ernesto's violin. Liesek helped himself to a set of strings that were lying around on the big table in the middle of the room.

'Heldermann won't notice,' Liesek said with a wink.

He did though, and he tacked the price onto the bill the next time Liesek needed to restring his bow.

Herr Heldermann wasn't Jewish but they still closed down his workshop because so many of the customers were. Heldermann seemed to crumble alongside his business and the last Ernesto heard, he fell down dead in the middle of the market place one sunny afternoon. What Ernesto remembered the most about the workshop was the smell, the powerful fragrance of smoke, sawdust and varnish. A smell he thought long dead when he was at Auschwitz but it soon reappeared and followed him to Buenos Aires. He couldn't remember what his plans were before the Nazis came to power but they certainly weren't to follow in Heldermann's footsteps.

However, after the gates of Auschwitz opened and he met a Russian for the first time, the disbelief of being alive still thundered over him every day and it filled too much of him to leave room for anything else for a long time. The disbelief subsided as the years went on and he could tremble with a nervous happiness on his wedding day and cry when his son, Sergio, was born.

He looked down at his hands, they weren't as gnarled and wrinkled as Heldermann's, but the lines had grown deeper, the veins were thicker and bluer. He hadn't noticed that before. He wiped his eyes with his right palm and pulled the letter out of his pocket but didn't read it, only put it down next to the violin and looked at it.

'It's me, Liesek,' the words made him cry out the first time he read it. The dead could come back to life, it seemed. 'I don't know if you remember me.' Liesek had written, and when Ernesto read that sentence, he dropped the letter and wrung his hands as if he were tugging at the lapels of Liesek's coat and shaking him. *'You think I've forgotten you?'*

The word Auschwitz stood out on the page and glittered a nasty sheen. Even the name of it blotted out Buenos Aires and he smelt the sweet, burning odour, saw the men in striped pyjamas, and heard the dogs barking. He was there again, now. His study didn't exist, or if it did, he wasn't there. He was standing on the black mud, playing Chopin's works with trembling fingers and watching the roll call. Every morning for two and a half years, he did it. Each man stepped forward when the guard barked out their name except those too weak, too tired to recognise it anymore. When that happened, someone dragged them away. At first, Ernesto assumed they were going to the infirmary. A year after he arrived, he discovered the truth. A truth which still collected the bile in the back of his throat. He put a hand to his mouth, repressing the burning sob there. Two and half years, he had inhaled the burning ash. Even now, the smell of cigarette smoke was the only thing that could block it out. He put both hands on the desk and let his shoulders drop a few inches.

From outside, the blare of city noises drifted through the air and he concentrated on them so he could remember where he was and where he wasn't. He picked up the packet for the 'D' strings and uncoiled one of them. D'Addario strings. Maybe Liesek hadn't played the violin since he left Auschwitz, but he would recognise a D'Addario string if he played one. Ernesto felt as if he were preparing a Christmas present.

Without warning, his vision blurred again and the string came to a dead end against the pegs and refused to coil around. 'Come on,' Ernesto said and for the first time, he realised how sour his mouth tasted. 'Come on.' He put the string down and watched it coil up on the table.

The letter stared at him with reproach. 'It's a chance in a million but do you still have my violin?' He had come straight to the point as he had always done. A few paragraphs down, he wrote something else that made Ernesto feel as if he had left Auschwitz the day before. 'Ernst, I dare allow myself the hope that you're still alive and that I haven't made a mistake or written to the wrong person. I've thought about you more than my own father. Can you imagine?'

When they arrived at the black gate with 'Arbeit Macht Frei' carved into the iron, the men in grey uniforms decided that Liesek would work and Ernesto would play the violin in the band. Unperturbed, Liesek pushed his violin into Ernesto's arms. 'Don't lose it,' he said before running off with the others. How he had managed to smuggle it onto the train, Ernesto couldn't imagine. Even when the dark-haired doctor questioned them all, examining them all closely, he didn't notice the violin propped up against the wall. He asked Ernesto how old he was.

'Twenty-one'

'Any lung diseases?'

'No, sir.'

'Any skin diseases?'

'Just scabies on my hands, sir.'

It went on like this for a few minutes before he moved onto the next man. Ernesto never saw the doctor again, only a photo of him in the newspaper when he died in Brazil in a boating accident. Camila tried desperately to get the newspaper out of the flat but he found it anyway. He read the article and realised with a jolt that, for some time, they had been in the same country. Two men escaping one history but for entirely different reasons. He tried not to think about it for too long though. Even now, the dark-haired doctor came back to him. Smiling, nodding at everyone as if the prisoners were something he wanted to buy. 'What do you do?' his voice as smooth as silk, he asked Ernesto the question twice.

'Violinist…Herr Doctor.'

'Violinist!' He seemed to savour the word in his mouth. 'Interesting.'

He, Liesek, and twenty others were told to go to the right and then they walked to a place called Auschwitz I. The others had to go left. What happened to them, Ernesto didn't find out until years later. Camila stood with the newspaper in her hand with diamond tears in her eyes as if Auschwitz were one of her bad memories, not his.

'Don't read it again,' she had never begged him for anything in their marriage before, only this, 'let me throw it away and we'll pretend we ever saw it.'

His insides were on fire and he had to stand up.

'Please do. Yes, throw it away.' He went to the bedroom so he could lie down for a bit. What he hated was the way she sobbed loudly as if she was trying to share his tragedy. If she had spent a minute there, she would hand back his suffering gladly even if he was her husband. Nobody would share those memories, the screams, the ash, the mud. Nobody would unburden a loved one of that agony. Nobody. He wanted to go out and yell in Camila's sweet face that she was a fool and a naïve one at that but he could never stay angry with her, not for long anyway. Nobody could. Everything about her, her hands, her hair, her skin were too soft and easily hurt. Even now when he was trying the fix the violin with hands and eyes that weren't obeying his commands, her sweet, violet smell was an almost imperceptible undertone.

He had finished the first two strings and he pulled the A string out of its packet. He could have strung twenty violins in the time it had taken him but he would keep going. Although his vision kept blurring and his left arm was a heavy, dead weight, he still had some feeling in the other hand. He kept Liesek's letter just in sight in case he felt ready to give up.

'I'll arrive in Buenos Aires on the 12th. I'm not sure what time but probably early in the morning. You don't have to meet me, but it would be wonderful if you could.'

The A string trembled in his hand. For two and a half years, he had waited for Liesek. Everyday with fingers burning from the cold, he waited for his name and the familiar figure to push its way forward from the neat rows of people. Every day, Liesek would acknowledge him, a look, a nod, even once, a wave and Ernesto could keep playing without the tightness in his belly. Liesek was alive, for one more day.

The musicians at Auschwitz had their own barracks and he had his own sack on the floor where he could be alone at night and think. Yes, for one more day, Liesek was alive. Others weren't so lucky. One night, the cellist discovered her mother was dead. Someone had seen her go off with a crowd of other women in striped coveralls to Block B-37. Ernesto didn't know what happened in this block but apparently the cellist did. The whole evening, she stared into space until she started screaming, and didn't stop. The other four musicians held her down and Ernesto stuffed a rag into her mouth. He hated himself for doing it but any disturbance was punishable by a beating. They waited until her screams turned into muffled sobs and let her go. Ernesto didn't try to comfort her, he didn't have any more comfort to give anyone. He could go back to his coarse sack and stare at the dirty, cracked ceiling and thank God one person, his friend, was safe. He looked up at the same ceiling every night and had the same thought.

Until that one day. The tightening coil in his stomach wound up further and further until the crowd thinned out to ten or eleven people, Liesek wasn't among them. His hand slid down the violin's neck making a bizarre almost comical slurring noise. Everyone turned to look, the guards, the prisoners, the other musicians, their faces barely visible in the early morning mist. He received a thrashing for that. The whole time, he clutched the commandant's ankles with his face in the mud. Despite the lashes, which were electric shocks of pain on his spine, the same question played around his head. 'Where's Liesek?'

'Don't worry,' Yurek, the cellist, told him, 'they've probably sent him to a work detail outside the wire.' He patted Ernesto's arm, Ernesto remembered the grey tufts of hair that poked out from his striped cap. He wanted to believe it and so he did. When Liesek didn't appear the next day, or the day after, he still believed it. He was at a work detail, probably living in better conditions too. Even when Yurek went to the infirmary with a chest infection and never came back, Ernesto still believed him.

The A string was in place now and Ernesto pulled out the last one from the packet. The E string was the finest and most difficult to feed through the loops. Shaking his head, he realised he should have started with this string. The coil tightened around his chest and the heaviness was spreading to his right wrist, he had the devil's work ahead of him as his mother used to say. He placed the dead weight of his arm on the violin's neck, fed the string through the bridge and pulled it. The breath was iron in his chest. He wanted to run. Pick up the violin and run to the port and will Liesek to come. He wouldn't care that the violin was unfinished and if he did, he wouldn't say anything. To see him, touch him, hear someone call him Ernst for the first time in thirty years, and hear him play the violin. Bach's sonata was their favourite. In the old days, they played until the early hours until someone came downstairs and told them to stop.

Seeing Liesek again, to bring back those days was the reality that had slowly faded over the years just as it had died the day the Russians arrived. They wanted to leave the camp immediately but relented when all the prisoners begged for time to look for any survivor.

Ernesto went from barrack to barrack, each one smelling of death and rot, and yelled out one name. Only a thick silence answered him. It didn't take anyone long, the prisoners soon met again at the black gate but they had to drag Ernesto out by the arms. He didn't remember much apart from the name he yelled to the sky and the rain that turned the ground to a thin, dark soup.

He knew he was sobbing when he tightened the E-string but the sobs were involuntary like a sneeze and he put a hand to his chest to stop them. His mouth tasted of pennies and the taste blossomed at the back of his throat when he leant forward and balanced the violin on his knees. Normally, he plucked strings with his left hand and turned the pegs with his right but now, his left arm was a wooden block without feeling and he laid it flat next to him and his right hand did all the work. Someone, something was pushing him back on the chair and he struggled to stay upright. A forest of strings and fingers floated in front of his eyes and he shook his head to regain focus.

'Come on,' he whispered to the violin. 'Work.'

Above the noise of the traffic, of Elvira rattling the crockery, the children running up and down the corridor upstairs, he heard Liesek's voice as clearly as if he were standing beside him at the black gate again. 'Take care of it,' he said when he pushed the violin into Ernesto's arms. Ernesto waited a few minutes in the rain and watched them take Liesek away. Yet, Liesek's name, which he had marked with pale chalk, was still there. Even after all this time, the 'L' was markedly visible despite the rain, despite the journey from Auschwitz to Buenos Aires and the twenty-five years buried out of sight in the cupboard. 'Take care of it.'

'I will.' Ernesto said to himself and kept going. The numbness was spreading down his left arm and his shoulder was beginning to spike with pain. His right hand reached out to massage his shoulder, but the violin nearly toppled off his lap and he stopped it just in time. He twanged the strings together, the melody was perfect. He leant forward and something crashed to the floor, when he pulled the violin case closer to the desk, broken glass tinkled over the floorboards.

'Are you OK, senor?' Elvira's voice called out.

'F-fine...fine,' he answered.

The next two seconds of silence pressed down on him until he nearly fell over. There was one more thing he had to do before he closed the violin case for the last time. In his drawer, there were four small blocks of rosin. 'Pirastro' was always the best one for Liesek's bow and through the blur in front of his eyes, he recognised the red box with white lettering. He took out the bow and balanced it on the table. By now, his vision had almost gone so he couldn't see the little screw to tighten the bow strings but after waving his right hand in the air for a few moments, he found it and turned it as much as his last iota of strength would allow. It was better to use long, sweeping motions to put rosin on a bow but Ernesto's hands were dead things attached to his arms so he could only work the rosin block up the bow with fidgety, little twitches.

When the air was bitter with rosin powder, he put the amber bar back in its box and put that in its right place in the drawer. With an air of finality, he loosened the strings on the bow, placed it next to the violin and closed the case. Through the milky haze that covered his eyes, he could make out its dark shape on the table. He picked it up and put it on the floor. In the drawer next to the rosin, was a bottle of alcohol and he took it out, gripping it between his thumb and forefinger. He let his hand drift around the desk for a minute before he felt a soft rag under his fingers. The bottle wouldn't open so he smashed it against the desk. He felt the cold splashes on his arms and chest. Careful not to touch the shards of glass, he dabbed the rag in the puddles on the floor and wiped as much of the case as he could, avoiding the area where Liesek's name was. A final motion and something twitched in his chest.

'Finished,' each syllable was a sharp kick to his throat.

He propped the case against wall behind him, careful to keep it out of the sun's rays. String instruments didn't do well in heat or out in the sun, something Herr Heldermann had told them. He fumbled for the fountain pen in his pocket. After finding a piece of paper and a dry patch on the desk, he wrote. His right hand only had enough feeling for a few lines.

Camila, On the 26th of July, a German immigrant called Liesek Denmer will arrive at Puerto Madero. Find him! Give him the violin. For everything we've been through, give him the violin.

With love,
Ernesto.

P.S. I did love you.

He could have written a lot more in the postscript but that was all his hand would allow. A warm wave, faster than a bolt of lightening swept down the centre of his body and he fell off his chair into the puddle of alcohol.

'Cam…Cami…Lisesk,' he whispered. He died a minute later. Camila and Sergio came home soon after. Elvira's wide eyes and open mouth told Camila that something was wrong and she hurried to the study. Unfortunately, the corner of the rug got caught on the door and she couldn't get it open. Camila fell to her knees.

'Ernesto,' her voice cracked, 'please.'

Her face contorted to an ugly shape and her light hair shook itself out of her tight bun. The whole time, she saw the sunlight fading through the crack in the door. Her screams brought Senor Puentes from upstairs running. Once he saw what was going on, he ran upstairs to fetch his little daughter and sent her through the crack in the door so she could flatten the rug and get the door open, with strict instructions not to look at Senor Grabo who had fallen on the floor.

Elvira ran to get Doctor de la Serna who came through the door looking grim. When he went into the study, Camila was sobbing on Ernesto's still chest. It took three of them to move her off him. Doctor de la Serna knew it was hopeless, but he massaged Ernesto's neck and looked at his watch to humour everyone. He looked up at Camila, Sergio, Elvira, and Senor Puentes and shook his head. By now, the doctor was immune to the screams of widows, parents, and orphans but even Camila's cries sent a minor tremor through him. On the way out, he recognised his daughter's violin case and took it downstairs. When he opened it, he was mildly irritated to see Ernesto hadn't had time to repair it.

Over the next few weeks, Elvira sent out a message to everyone who had left their violin with Ernesto to come and collect them. Any that were unclaimed, she donated to the university choir. The day they sent someone to collect them was hot and unpleasant, the driver piled them onto the back of a truck he had borrowed and wiped the sweat off his forehead. On the way to the music faculty, he swerved to avoid a cat and one the violins fell out onto the road.

The week after, the President elect gave his address. Those who didn't take to the streets to protest stayed at home and debated whether to leave the country. Most of the German immigrants decided it wouldn't be the same as 1933 and were relieved. All the while, another German immigrant was at the Puerto Madero, watching and waiting. When the clock in the central hall struck seven, he left but came back the next day. And the day after, and the day after.

SIMON ROWE

Simon Rowe grew up in small town New Zealand and big city Australia. His stories have appeared in TIME (Asia), The Paris Review, The New York Times, and The Australian Financial Review. He is the author of *Good Night Papa: Short Stories from Japan and Elsewhere (2017)*, and his most recent short story, *The Convenience Store Ballerina*, appears in The Best Asian Short Stories 2019 anthology. He was a Finalist, Hollyshorts Film Festival Los Angeles, U.S., for the short screenplay *The Girl From Pearl City (2016)* and *The Foonabiki Barbers (2015)* . And winner of The Paris Review, *Windows on the World* essay competition (2014), New York, U.S.

When not writing short fiction, he tends to his blog about life in a traditional Japanese neighbourhood, *www.mightytales.net/ seaweed-salad-days.*

HIGHLY-COMMENDED
OUEN PRESS
SHORT STORY COMPETITION 2019

NIGHT FISHING
by Simon Rowe

'Stringbean' Riggs jiggled his cup and drained the gin to the rocks. He peered out of the window, first at the clouds, then at the earth, wondering if the lush and otherworldly island beneath him was Cebu or just another green jewel in the Visayan Sea.

The plane dropped like an elevator. A woman gasped. The old man in the seat behind uttered a *Hail Mary* and Riggs thought he heard Rosary beads chatter. Presently the cabin attendants appeared, the prayers subsided, and passengers took comfort in the bored faces of the two young women who seated themselves in the bulkhead facing them.

Riggs crushed an ice cube between his teeth. He scratched the nub of pink skin where his left hand used to be, and caught one of the attendants watching.

She smiled quickly and said, 'First time to the Philippines?'

'No,' he said.

'On holiday?'

'Sort of.'

'Staying long on Cebu?'

'That depends.'

She smiled again, but it was purely professional. Riggs didn't feel much like small talk; his attention drifted back to the window and the sugarcane fields and mango tree plantations which grew greener and more voluminous as the plane descended. He glimpsed a lorry, a cane truck perhaps, crawling beetle-like along a dusty highway towards a hamlet in the distance. So different to the dishwater-grey sprawl of London, now twenty-two hours behind him.

He felt his armpits leaking. The gin had worn off and the unease had crept back. It was the same deep, ominous feeling he'd felt opening the small brown envelope which had dropped through the mail slit of his flat five weeks earlier. Five postage stamps of General Douglas MacArthur and 'Mister Allan Riggs' scrawled in a curious hand across the creased, travel-worn paper. He touched his chest pocket, confirming that the letter with the Polaroid photograph were still in his possession. In less than forty-eight hours he would be standing face to face with its sender. The stains at his armpits grew darker.

The pilot banked and in a wide arc brought the aircraft's nose into the wind. The sea lay below them, whitecaps whipped by the wind and racing to shore. The plane came in low and uneven across the outer reef, skimming the turquoise lagoon, until the land reared up in a green blur and flight PI420 kissed the hot tarmac of Cebu island.

Like MacArthur, Riggs had returned. He hadn't planned to. In fact, he had vowed *not* to after what had happened in Angeles City seventeen years earlier. He half-expected the immigration officer to say, 'Mister Allan Riggs? We have been expecting you, would you please step this way.' Or, from the gallery of glistening faces on the other side of the arrival hall doors, 'Welcome back Stringbean, you crazy sonofabitch!'

For better or for worse, time works its magic on a man; widening his girth, thinning his pate, shrinking his gums, leeching him of testosterone... No-one recognised him as he moved through the immigration corrals, the customs gates, then out into the arrivals hall. He was just another tall, balding *dayuhan,* with one good hand and a duffel bag, moving solemnly and sluggishly through the concourse throngs to the taxi stand.

'Sampaguita Guesthouse? Legaspi Street? Yeah, I know it,' the driver said, casting his cigarette to the ground. 'Seventy pesos. Get in.'

They drove in silence, through the cane fields, then the industrial parks, passing the sun-bleached slums of the city limits, until they reached a traffic signal and the driver stopped to wind down the window and dispatch a wad of phlegm onto the steaming asphalt.

'Know what Sampaguita means?' he said, wiping his mouth.

'Jasmine,' said Riggs.

'Means Jasmine. *Jasmine Guesthouse.*'

'I know,' Riggs said.

'First time to Cebu?'

'No.'

'You want marijuana?'

'No.'

'You want girl?'

'No. I want to sleep.'

'You want to sleep with girl?'

'I want to sleep till I'm dead.'

'Dead no good for business. I bring girl and marijuana to Jasmine Guesthouse tomorrow, okay?'

Riggs rubbed the stump of his wrist; the heat made it tingle. He watched the crazed choreography of bikes, buses and Jeepneys swirl past. He glimpsed the roadside fry-stalls and juice stands, mangy dogs and half-naked kids roaming between them, and everywhere people talking, smoking, drinking and laughing. Were people who lived near the equator happier than those who lived near the poles? Did cheerful poverty trump miserable wealth? Could *he* call a place like this 'home'? Time would tell.

'What happen to your hand?' the driver asked.

Riggs glanced at the rear vision mirror. The driver's greasy face gleamed in the late afternoon sun.

'Lost it in Saudi Arabia,' Riggs said.

The driver shot him a quizzical look, but said nothing until they reached the periphery of the old town. There, he turned off the main road and into a narrow tree-lined street. Outside an elegant colonial-era building with a purple bougainvillea vine cascading over its iron gate, he pulled up and cut the engine.

'Eighty pesos,' he said.

'You said seventy,' said Riggs.

'I burn rubber to get here.'

Riggs reached beneath his trouser belt and wrestled with his crotch. The driver's eyes narrowed, watching the *dayuhan* pull from between his legs a fistful of damp pesos and throw them onto the front seat.

'Cut your hand off,' Riggs said.

'What?'

'For stealing in Saudi Arabia. They cut off your hand.' He took his bag and exited the car, leaving the driver to utter a Cebuano curse word and count his money.

The guesthouse lobby was cool and dim-lit. Riggs' nose twitched at a familiar scent. He searched the room for its source, spotted the floral arrangement at the end of the teakwood counter, and leaned down to fill his nostrils.

'You like Arabian jasmine, Sir?' the elderly receptionist enquired.

'I'm a gardener,' Riggs said, scrawling his name into the guest register and pocketing his key. 'Thank you.'

The upstairs room overlooked the street. A desk, a ceiling fan, a small bed, and a painting of a woman combing her hair beside a waterfall were its only comforts. After sluicing himself, he put on a fresh shirt and bought two cans of San Miguel from reception. He must have passed out because when awoke, sounds of laughter and pop music drifted up from the street. From the window, Riggs peered down onto dozens of mobile kitchens which had sprung up along the tree-lined thoroughfare. Night had wrapped the city in a suffocating stillness and its fragrant fug pressed in on him as he left the guesthouse in search of food. Sodium lamps dangled from the trees, casting a warm glow over the tables where Cebuanos sat laughing, drinking and gorging themselves. Riggs stopped to watch a woman carving a roast suckling piglet. He took a seat, ordered a beer, and the *lechon* arrived soon after, sliced thickly and piled high on a plastic plate. He ate the succulent meat hungrily.

'Scuze me, mate,' said a voice behind him. Riggs turned to find a gaunt foreigner standing over him. He wore faded shorts, his eyes were bloodshot and jaundiced, and his chest bones pushed through his batik shirt like an old washboard.

'You American?' the man asked.

'British,' Riggs replied.

'Been here long?'

'Couple of hours.'

'Staying?'

'Maybe.'

The man considered Riggs for moment, then his gaze fell to the suckling pig. He pulled out a stool and sat down. 'Listen mate, I'm in a bit of a tight spot…'

Riggs chewed his mouthful, waiting – the best storytellers in the world were Australians.

'Some cunt stole me wallet while I was in the shower this mornin'. Bastard cleaned me out like a Kolcatta curry...'

Riggs swallowed his mouthful and washed the gristle down with beer. 'How much?'

'I'm not begging, mate. I'm not one of those shitty *begpackers* you see everywhere.'

'How much do you need?'

The man gripped the table and leaned closer, his voice falling to a desperate whisper. 'I gotta get outta here, mate. I gotta get to Manila.'

Riggs looked about at the families and office workers clustered at the makeshift tables, enjoying their dinner beneath a constellation of tiny light bulbs. He looked back at the man's face and saw something he recognised. It was fear. Fear of dying, fear of living, fear of never finding peace? He wasn't sure, but he had seen that look in a mirror.

'How much do you need to get to Manila?'

'Can you spare a coupla thousand?'

Riggs put down his fork. He slipped his hand beneath his belt and pulled out two one-thousand peso notes which he laid on the table. The man's fingers trembled as he raked the money towards him, reminding Riggs of an old skeleton money box he'd owned as a kid.

'Preciate this, mate. Really do,' the man said, rolling the bills into a tube and holding them tightly. He extended his other hand. 'Barry's the name.'

'Allan,' Riggs said, and their greasy palms locked together.

'Gimme your address Allan. I'll pay you back.'

'Forget it.'

'Nah-nah, I'm not gunna forget it, mate. Gimme your address and I'll send you the money from Manila.'

'Just do the same for someone else in need and we'll call it even.' Riggs called over the stall owner and paid the bill.

'Here, write it down,' the man persisted, pulling a chewed Biro from somewhere and taking a tissue from the dispenser. 'C'mon, mate.'

As Riggs scribbled, the man mouthed the words, '*Stringbean Riggs, London Royal Parks...*'

'Best of luck, Barry.'

'Geez mate, what happened to your hand?'

But Riggs did not reply. He was on the move, weaving between the tables of lively diners, putting distance between himself and what he might have become seventeen years ago had a sympathetic Australian not helped him.

'Stringbean! Mate, I'm gunna get that money to ya!' the man yelled, loud enough for diners to turn and glance in his direction. Had Riggs looked back, he'd have seen the Australian slump down at the table and start hand-sifting his greasy leftovers.

o0o

Riggs lay half-naked beneath the ceiling fan with the letter fluttering against his hand. The contents he knew by heart. The pure, simple sentences – childlike in construction, earnest in intention – had shaken him to his core. He picked up the Polaroid and held it to the bedside lamp light, studying the face of the figure which gazed awkwardly back at him. He'd scoured the recesses of his mind for the name 'Cruz' but could not recall anyone he'd met in Angeles City by that name. Yet, the familiarity was unmistakable; it had left him sleepless and agitated, night after night, day after day, until he'd been able to stand it no longer. He took leave of his job, paid his rent two months in advance and bought an air ticket to the other side of the world.

One day a groundsman for the Royal Parks of London, tilling horse manure and talking peonies with lonely old women; next, a middle-aged man adrift, holed up in a cheap hotel in the Philippines, awaiting a dawn bus to carry him north to a boat that will ferry him across the Visayan Sea to an island where someone who represents his past, present, and possibly his future, awaits.

He returned the photo and the letter to his money belt, set his alarm, and turned off the light.

o0o

In the dawn light, a bus terminal vendor sold him a cup of steaming coffee and a banana pancake. As the sun fingered the tops of the office towers, the bus passed out through the shanties and joined the Grand Nautical Highway heading north. Though hidden from view by dense roadside foliage, the sea made its presence known on the cool, briny air that rushed in through the bus's open windows.

Curled up against each other, the older passengers availed themselves to the rhythm of the road and were soon dozing. The younger ones let their gaze wander the landscape, perhaps thinking of the family and friends awaiting them at the end of line, or of those left behind.

The bus veered inland, passing ramshackle villages and flooded rice paddies where farmers sat smoking, watching their water buffalo graze. Seventeen years earlier, on a bus from Manila to Angeles City, Riggs had been too drunk to see anything but the smashed insects on the window pane. Now the landscape beguiled him. He marvelled at the size, colour and variation of its flora: the fiery red flowers of the dap-dap tree, the cream-white blossoms of the bani tree which spread like a huge umbrella over the highway, the rampaging hibiscus – all so different to the delicate, manicured gardens of England.

When they stopped for breakfast at a roadhouse, Riggs joined the mêlée at the buffet, piling his plate with pancit noodles and adobo chicken, adding two cans of San Miguel to ease his nerves and drawing knowing smiles from the older men. When he climbed back aboard the bus, the seat beside his had been taken. The young Filipino introduced himself as Vincent. He wore a white business shirt and pressed trousers, and his white teeth flashed when he spoke.

'You're going to Maya?' he asked.

'Yes,' said Riggs.

'There's nothing in Maya. So, I guess you're going to Malapascua Island?'

'Yes.'

'Beautiful place. The water is so clear, you get dizzy just looking down. Your first time?'

'Yes.'

'You're a scuba diver?'

'No.'

The man looked at him curiously. 'But there's nothing else to do there.'

'That's why I'm going.'

The man smiled, but his eyes failed to hide his puzzlement. He changed the subject and for a while Riggs, politely as he could, kept their conversation to hometowns, jobs and the weather in England. He learned that the man was an English teacher in a small village school, and that he was fulfilling his Board of Education training to work for one year in a remote rural area of Cebu.

'I miss my family,' the teacher said. 'You're married?'

'No.'

'But you have family in London, don't you?'

'No.'

'No brothers or sisters?'

Riggs shook his head.

'I'm sorry to hear that. Filipino families are big… Many brothers and sisters. We say children are a gift from God.' He flashed his teeth.

Riggs returned a smile, but his gaze returned to the world of light and colour beyond the window. He thought of his mother and father, worm-eaten and brittle beneath the cold turf of London Cemetery, and a feeling of melancholy overcame him. He hadn't exactly been their gift from God; his reckless ways had driven his mother to tears and his father to kick him out of home on his eighteenth birthday. By twenty he was squatting in a south London flat and peddling Moroccan hashish to west London rich kids.

The bus descended onto a plain and a vast plantation of sugarcane stretched before them. The asphalt faded to coral dust and soon the passengers and their possessions were covered in a fine grey powder. When a small farming town appeared and the bus drew into its clapboard roadhouse, the teacher rose from his seat and said, 'This is my stop.' He took his Boston bag from the rack and shook Riggs' hand. 'Sorry to be rude, but I've been meaning to ask… How did you lost your hand?'

'Scuba diving,' Riggs said.

'That's what I thought!' The teacher nodded vigorously. 'I tell my students – humans are land creatures. We don't belong in the water. Me, I can't even swim!' He flashed a smile, the doors closed after him and the bus lurched away.

Ruffled by the dry breeze, the sugarcane fields rolled on in endless design. Riggs extended his legs, glad for the extra space and the absence of an inquiring gaze. He pulled the letter from his chest pocket and re-read the sender's instructions one more time; then, resting his head against the rattling windowside, he fell asleep.

He awoke to a furnace blast in his face. The hot gust whipped the letter from his fingers and sent it flying out the window, fluttering up into the dust clouds. His first impulse was to dash to the driver and ask him to stop. But the request would have sounded absurd and he slumped back gloomily in his seat.

They sailed on through the sea of green, the bus tossing its passengers this way and that, until the growl of the engine abruptly ceased and Riggs felt the vehicle drifting to a stop on a long stretch of desolate highway. The driver announced that the engine had lost power and that there would be a delay. Outside, Riggs kicked at the dust. He looked about at the old men with tired eyes, the drowsy teenagers sipping warm Coke, and the giggling women who disappeared into the sugarcane to relieve themselves. He felt out of his depth – a one-handed, middle-aged English gardener treading water in the deep, slow-moving torrent of humanity that was not his own. Gazing out onto the endless fields of sugarcane and the long, white ribbon of coral dust that shimmered behind him, he felt a crushing solitude. He had no idea what to do.

At the rear of the bus he found the driver wrestling with the bus's innards. A snapped drive belt lay like a dead snake in the dust at his feet. Riggs recalled what a workshop mechanic had once told him and said, 'Pantyhose.'

The driver looked up, first at Riggs' face, then at his missing hand.

'What did you say?'

'Ladies's pantyhose. You can use them as a drive belt until you get to a garage.'

The driver chuckled. 'You want to ask around?' He gestured to the middle-aged and elderly women squatting in the shade of the bus, then returned to his tinkering, leaving Riggs to search the cloudless sky for an answer. It was now late afternoon. With Maya several hours away, he worried that he might not make the ferry.

A plume of dust rose in the distance. In a short while, a convoy of cane lorries emerged from the heat mirage. When the lead truck drew alongside the bus, its sun-blackened driver thrust out his head and exchanged words with the bus driver. Phone calls were made, and then came an announcement. Riggs found himself hoisted up by a burly cane cutter and into the walled tray of an ancient Fuso. There he squatted with a dozen others as the lorry lurched forward and resumed its northward journey. The roar of the engine and the swirling cane chaff rendered all communication pointless, so passengers took refuge in their own private thoughts and prayers, hopeful, like Riggs, that they would reach Maya by nightfall.

The hours passed and the air grew more humid. Plots of tilled farmland and ramshackle homes with groves of mango trees and fishing nets slung between them appeared. Passengers shook off the dust and rose to their feet to put their faces to the warm, salty breeze. A scruffy port town emerged in the distance, and like a plain of brushed silver the Visayan Sea stretched beyond it.

Inside the Maya-Malapascua Ferry Office, Riggs bought a one-way ticket and a Coke. He rolled the bottle against his wrist, soothing the itchiness, until an ancient Tannoy speaker crackled to life and a sleepy female voice announced that the ferry was ready for boarding.

It was an outrigger with stabilisers which spread like albatross wings, and a blue canvas awning under which passengers crowded with their belongings. The engine belched and grunted, the propellor churned the brine to a green froth and the ferry pushed out into the lagoon. Riggs sat near the bow, happy to leave behind him the hot breath of the land. He scanned the horizon and saw nothing but the melding of sea with sky. Now and again, flying fish broached the surface and winged ahead of them. He felt someone touch his arm and turned to find an elderly woman pointing out to sea. 'Turtle,' she said, indicating a huge creature whose head bobbed for a few moments then quickly dived.

The thrum of the propellor and rocking motion of the boat as it slipped through the velveteen swell held the passengers in a strange hypnosis. Darkness crept across the Visayan Sea, so that only the lights of fishing boats scuttling back and forth on the horizon were visible. Again, he felt the woman touch his arm. 'Malapascua,' she said, pointing to a tiny cluster of lights peeping above the skyline. 'You come for the festival?' she asked.

'What festival?'

'Lawihan, the Thresher Shark Festival. It's tomorrow, you know. Everywhere boats coming from other islands, music, a parade, and roast pig – lots of *lechon!* You like *lechon*?'

He nodded, his gaze unshifting from the lights ahead. Soon, the propeller's rhythm slowed and the bow wash flattened. Riggs strained to see the lay of the land ahead. The moon had risen, silhouetting a small hillock at one end, and below this a white sand beach rimmed a crescent-shaped cove. Coconut palms studded it's shore and a single building stood with a light shining above it. The scent of the land drifted out to greet them, causing Riggs' nostrils to twitch; he smelled jasmine.

The captain throttled down, manoeuvring the ferry between vessels moored in the cove, and the deckhands rushed forward to ready the gangway. Passengers in jeans rolled them to their knees; those in skirts hitched them into their underwear. The ferry's keel pushed into the sand, and after the gangplank had been lowered, passengers splashed ashore with their boxes and cartons held high. Riggs watched as the whole procession moved past the boat house and up a sandy path through the coconut palms. He stood alone on the damp sand, his shoes in one hand, his duffel bag in the crook of his other arm. His stump itched terribly. Save for the crew, who now busied themselves securing the ferry, the beach was completely deserted. A horrible thought flashed through his mind that he had landed on the wrong island. But no, the old woman had been right—a sign above the boatshed announced, 'Malapascua Island Ferry Co.'

He followed the sandy path which the others had taken. From the top of the knoll he stood looking down on a sprawling village with tin rooftops glinting in the moonlight. Somewhere a rooster crowed and a child cried. He soon found himself on a sandy street lined with shop houses, each one festooned with paper flowers and Tanduay Rum flags which fluttered in the light breeze. He stopped outside one, a bar of sorts, with tables scattered across its sandy forecourt where a few old timers were drinking beer and playing Fan Tan. They glanced up from their card game and Riggs noted a curious recognition in their faces, as if they had been expecting him. 'Anna!' one of them called. Through the shop's open door a middle-aged woman appeared. She had a large, welcoming face and wore a pink T-shirt with a Rolling Stones tongue stretched across her breasts. When she saw Riggs, her eyes widened. She rushed forward.

'Mister Riggs?'

'Yes?' he said.

'We thought you weren't coming,' she said breathlessly. '*Thank you* for coming.'

'My bus broke down...'

'Ronnie's been waiting. He thought you'd changed your mind.'

'Where is he?'

She turned and shouted something through the door. Two young boys appeared, barefoot and wearing soccer uniforms. She spoke quickly in Tagalog and the youths stared wide-eyed, first at Riggs' missing hand, then at his face. 'My sons will take you to him. He's out on the reef, fishing for octopus.' She stepped closer and held out her hand. 'I'm Anna Cruz, Ronnie's aunt. Gracie was my older sister. We worked together in Angeles City.'

It was the moment Riggs had been dreading; when his past would fly up into his face and slap him publicly. *Actions have consequences.* 'I'm so sorry for your loss. I'm sure she was a good mother to Ronnie,' was all he could muster.

'He was all she had. She didn't tell him about you until just before she passed away. She was proud and stubborn and we all loved her,' she said, her eyes glistening in the lamp light.

'Ronnie found me on the internet?'

'You must have given Gracie your address. My eldest son found a photo of you online. You won a gardening contest in London…'

'A long time ago.'

She smiled with delight. 'Go on, Carlos and Joshua will take you to him. He'll be so happy.' She wiped her cheeks. 'Leave your bag. Go!'

The moon hung large and full and set the coral sand beach at the end of the street aglow with its brightness. A king tide had emptied the lagoon like a kitchen sink and far out across the shallow water, all the way to the reef's foaming edge, lanterns drifted back and forth like glowing sentinels. These, the boys said, were the octopus hunters.

'Wait, please,' the oldest boy told Riggs. He scampered across the sand and waded into the lagoon until only his silhouette was visible against the moonlight reflected in the water. A short while later, one of the lanterns ceased moving. Riggs' heartbeat quickened. His nerves tightened. He sucked on the briny air with short rapid breaths.

Actions have consequences. One night a man walks into a bar in Angeles City. Blind on drink, he is beguiled by a beautiful Filipina. One night in her company turns into a week and he blows all of his money on uppers and downers and everything in between to keep the fantasy alive – and almost dies trying. He wakes up in a police cell, bloodied and half-naked, with charges of public indecency and assaulting another dayuhan to his name. Then, from somewhere steps an Australian, an older, wiser man whose face he's never seen before, or can't recall, who posts bail and puts the foolish young man on a bus to Manila and a flight home.

'Did a shark do that?' said the youngest boy. Riggs caught him staring at his pink stump, and the earnestness in the boy's face recalled his own childhood, when life's mysteries were many and answers few.

'You climb coconut trees?' he asked the boy.

'Uh-huh.'

'Are you careful?'

'Why?'

'Because one day I climbed a tree with a chainsaw in my hands, and I wasn't.'

Riggs could not know what he was thinking or whether he had even understood. A sudden cry rang out from across the water and the lantern began to move towards them. Riggs stepped to the water's edge. He felt the cool water wash over his feet, but his body felt on fire. The lantern grew nearer and soon a tall, slim youth slowly emerged in its glow.

'Hello Ronnie,' said Riggs.

The teenager's eyelids flickered. A shy smile fought its way onto his lips as he stepped onto the wet sand. Then, from his mouth came a sound which was neither Tagalog nor English, but another language which Riggs had heard from time to time in the parks and streets of London.

'Ronnie don't speak,' said the younger boy.

The teenager gestured with his hands and the boy said, 'He says, hello.' But it was Riggs who was lost for words; he could not pull his gaze from the long legs, the finely-muscled shoulders, the strong cheekbones and soft gaze of the person standing before. The teenager from the Polaroid – in the flesh. *Riggs' own flesh.*

Worry flashed across the young man's face. He signed quickly and the boy translated: 'Ronnie says he's sorry.'

'For what?' said Riggs.

'For not telling you.'

'Not telling me what?'

'That he doesn't speak. He was worried you wouldn't come. He's very happy...'

Riggs sensed a huge weight shifting from his shoulders. He felt his head growing light, as if into the void were rushing seventeen years of lost time. No matter that they spoke different languages; no matter that they were both missing things which others took for granted. Neither of them seemed to notice the other's disability.

'Tell him I'm happy too,' he said, outstretching his hand.

But as the young man stepped forward to grasp it, Riggs pulled the teenager to his chest and held him tightly. The reek of salt, sweat and octopus did not register. He felt only the warmth of a familial embrace and it was the most electrifying sensation he had ever known.

'Ronnie wants to know if you like octopus?' said the eldest boy, stepping forward and holding up the bucket. 'Barbecue tonight.'

Riggs looked down at the tangle of grey, writhing tentacles and said, 'You'll need more than five.'

The young man smiled broadly. He had somehow understood. He jerked his head towards the reef, signed a message to them all, then picked the lantern.

'Ronnie says, octopus don't jump into buckets by themselves. Let's go fishing!'

RHONDA COLLIS

Rhonda Collis is a Canadian from Oliver, British Columbia, the daughter of a teacher and RCMP officer whose work during her childhood required relocating every few years, from BC, to Saskatchewan, Alberta and finally, Ontario. At the University of British Columbia, Vancouver, she gained an MFA. Rhonda has worked jobs in office administration, magazine publishing, broadcasting, human resources, and technical writing. But it wasn't until her two daughters started school that she pursued writing fiction and poetry seriously, returning to the University of Victoria to participate in undergrad writing workshops with numerous renowned poetry instructors.

Her writing has won awards from *Room, The Fiddlehead, The Antigonish Review* and *The New Quarterly* magazines. Her fiction and poetry has also been published in *On Spec, Smartish Pace, ARC, MsLexia, Freefall, Comstock Review, Prairie Fire* and various anthologies in Canada and the UK.

She now lives on her acreage with her husband, north of Victoria on rural Vancouver Island, where she writes and teaches ESL (or ESOL) at the Cowichan Intercultural Association. Online, she can be found at rhondacollis.com.

HIGHLY-COMMENDED
OUEN PRESS
SHORT STORY COMPETITION 2019

KREEGER
by Rhonda Collis

In the condominium's orange lobby light I stand between the doors like a fish in an aquarium. I run fingertips over my sandpaper cheeks and squint at the dark recesses in the nooks and crannies fronting the building. I can't see Kreeger tonight. Most evenings, he squats at the door, his cap in his hand, as familiar to me as the potted split-leaved plant or the smoked glass mirror in the condo foyer.

I pull the door open, breaking the suction of the rubber seal. The cold wind sucks out the warmth. The lawn is slick, and I almost wipe out in the puddles of sloppy snow as I walk to the far corner of the building. Halfway down the long wall in the bottomless black shadow, something rustles. Once my eyes have adjusted, I see a large dark mound moving beneath a dryer vent's hum of hot air. I take a few steps and call Kreeger's name. That's all it takes for my old friend to emerge from a buckling tarp. Regardless of how his shoulders have sunk forward, he's still broad-chested with the sagging remnants of what used to be muscle. Maybe once upon a time he was a soldier or something. He greets me like a general with a few clipped words and an angry muttering or two. I return the greeting self-consciously as if I'm some kind of zookeeper offering steak, although I don't have anything near as nourishing as steak. Often, I have nothing more than a couple of bucks.

'I'm going out. Just wanted to wish you an uneventful night.' I jingle keys and coins in my pocket, looking for the weight of something more substantial than nickels and dimes. Disappointed, I flex my fingers into my gloves and think about how I shouldn't eat out so often. Tomorrow I'll start looking up recipes on the internet. Mom and Naani might have taught me to cook if it weren't for my father's declaration, '*there's no need for that, he'll find a wife who can cook for him.'* From time to time my parents call long distance or email the names and profiles of single women they know, as if they still live in India and can arrange a marriage for me. So many time zones away, they still bristle over my indifference.

Without making eye contact, Kreeger shambles over and hands me a stash of crumpled brochures, coupons and flyers from inside his coat, then huddles back against the white stucco wall. He always hands me some of the junk mail he's collected for the day. In his own way he's an archivist, like I am, except that his efforts at collecting data bring immediate results.

Because of his flyers, I often find new restaurants or save money with promotional offers. I'm envious, though, because he collects his information from the hands of the living, like hawkers, instead of reaching into the world of ghosts like I do.

I imagine Kreeger's footsteps wandering downtown Victoria – under the hanging flower baskets on Government Street – from one restaurant to the next, collecting his treasury of brochures. He plods on, oblivious to the annoyed or uncomfortable glances from tourists who eat their Rogers chocolates while searching the Inner Harbour for totem poles and whale watching tours. There he is plucking one from the sweaty kid wearing a sandwich-board advertising Beacon Hill Bangers & Mash. When he gets tired, I see him resting awhile on Douglas Street, an inverted hat on the sidewalk in front of him. Then, when the sun dips behind the buildings, he drags his hobbled rusted shopping cart the five blocks along Fort Street, and three blocks south to the relative safety and obscurity of my condo building's somewhat neglected lawns.

I coax Kreeger out of his huddle beside the dryer vent, onto the sidewalk. One large boot, then the other, laces missing, plant themselves before me. Still in a crouch, his grimy hand thrusts at me his offering for the evening. Under the yellow streetlight, I shake tiny snowflakes from a slick black and red job, advertising the opening of a new restaurant, Cheap Eats. Sounds like my kind of place. I flip it over for the address.

'This one's close by,' I say.

'So's the end of the world.' Kreeger doesn't face me when he speaks. He continues to look at the ground while he sings and sways.

Late November's first snowfall is coming hard now, sliding under the collar of my coat. The cold takes me back to last December and The Blizzard of '96. Victoria's limited snow-clearing equipment couldn't keep up with it and the streets were a mess. I'd given Kreeger a sleeping bag. I couldn't sleep so I came out to the balcony at midnight to see him burrowed under the layers of quilted nylon beside his cart. Usually, by that time, the cops had chased him away but, I guess because of the weather, they'd had other things to do. I should have rescued him, but I didn't have the courage. I must have stood on my balcony's bone-chilling concrete for twenty minutes although it seemed a lot longer. I could've put shoes on but I wanted to feel the kind of cold he felt, the kind that shoots up from your heels. I wasn't going anywhere until I'd seen the men in blue chase the old codger to a warmer place. My bare feet were numb by the time they finally arrived.

'Have at it. Go ahead. Have at it.' Kreeger shakes his fist at the snow. 'You won't be staying long. God damned bastards.'

'Hey, buddy, take it easy. Deep breaths, my man.'

Though Kreeger knows my face, and might even know my daily routine. Though I've told him my name several times, he asks again.

I thrust out my hand as if it's the first time, 'I'm Shameed.'

'Okay, Mr. Shameed. Okay.' Kreeger ignores my hand and gives me a gruff clap on the shoulder.

The glossy brochure seems to shiver in the cold. The photos of the inside of the restaurant appear warm, kind of homey. A quick reno job on an old building, nothing too fancy. A family smiles from a booth; the waitresses are clad in gingham; there's a close-up photo of starchy fresh-baked breads and thick soups. Not exactly Tandoori Chicken but something I imagine Kreeger would like.

I hold up the brochure and point to the picture as if it's a teaching aid of some kind.

'Come with me,' I say with a mysterious new-found confidence.

Kreeger squints as if I'm speaking a foreign language.

'Here,' I say louder and point to the photograph of a table of smiling people, forks raised.

Kreeger's head rears back as if some invisible force is reefing on it. His eyes dart one direction, then the next. The air around him becomes charged.

I take a step back. 'Never mind,' I say. 'Just an idea. It's cold out here.' I feel idiotic listening to myself speak; it's probably cold every night of his life. I'm a moron sometimes. I turn and walk away.

It's the squeal and grating of the shopping cart wheels behind me that cause me to look back. The cart lurches from side to side with Kreeger at the helm – some kind of grey-feathered ghoul. Despite the steering challenges he has no problem catching up to me. The few people on the sidewalk give him a wide berth, staring through the thickening snow. The cart is filled with green garbage bags and white plastic bags. Striped canvas sacks are tied on the grilled sides and on the handle bar. Sheathes of cardboard plank out from the bottom shelf. I feel lighter and happier now that he's come up beside me, but heavier with every thump of the cart. I grab the front corner to steady it.

'Kreeger, we're not going to be gone long. Can't you leave this behind?'

'Thieves'll get it, crazy bugger. Thieves.'

He looks over one shoulder and then the other. He ducks his head and covers it with folded arms as if comets are crashing to earth.

'Listen, relax, we'll take your cart. The place should be just up here.' I try to ignore the stares, and am glad for the cover of night and falling snow, as difficult as the accumulation makes it to manoeuvre the cart's small sticky wheels.

'Maybe you know them thieves.'

It's more a summation than a question.

'Nothing personal, but none of the thieves I know would want your stuff, Kreeger.'

'Huh.' He shrugs. That seems to offer comfort and makes him slow down to think. 'They'd want the money. All that gold and silver you give me.'

'Yeah, they want everybody's money.' I grin at him. 'You could call them thieves or crooks or, hey, maybe even the government.'

'Goddamned government,' Kreeger mutters. 'They take it out of your teeth. Climb on your chest in the night and squeeze your heart until you can't move and take all your silver from you.'

He rams into my ankles in an effort to get through a stubborn clump of snow. I wince and curse, then put a controlling hand on the front grill. Together, we gather momentum and have the thing wobble-rolling its way through the slush and snow and some puddles when Kreeger stops.

'Not going there.' His voice is unsteady. 'Can't

make me, mister.'

I yank on the front top rim of the cart but he's got a killer grip on his end. 'Come on.'

'Go too far and there's no turning back, dumb ass.'

'Right.' I release the cart, throw up my arms. 'Fine. You don't want a nice warm cup of coffee, a hot meal of potatoes and steak, a thick slice of pie, that's your choice. Just trying to be nice here.'

I walk on for what seems like a few minutes before I hear his voice again.

'Hey! Hey wait, dog breath, wait.'

I turn and he stops, but not before I get an eyeful of his strange shuffling lope. The black and white hunchback movies come back to me; the series of old zombie flicks I watched and re-watched, anything with, living dead, in the title – Diary of the Living Dead, Land of – , Day of –, Dawn of – , Night of the Dead. Well steeped in horror as a kid, I watched every remake of Frankenstein.

'It's just that everything might break up. It could all break up around me and then I'll be all gone,' Kreeger says.

I look ahead and spot the lit green restaurant sign a few buildings away. I point to it. 'Look it's right there. We can see it. Bring your stuff. I'll help you.'

I'm careful not to rush him or talk too much. He mutters constantly, calling everything he passes a name, and cursing at it. I want to rip through the green plastic garbage bag to find out more about him, dig down past all his paraphernalia to the bottom of the cart to know why he's so crazy, although I know that sleeping in the rain on cold concrete night after night, depending on guys like me for food and drink, nowhere to take a decent shit, would make me crazy too.

During one of my many bouts of insomnia last February, I got up for a glass of water and went to the balcony. There was Kreeger rolling across the sidewalk in the sleeping bag I'd given him, the price tags I'd forgotten to remove flapping like little grey flags as he turned. I looked for any other lights on in the building but it was dark. Kreeger kept talking as he rotated and finally wedged himself under a bench, then fell silent.

I went inside, finished my water, got a blanket off my bed and wrapped it around me. Maybe it was in the interest of solidarity that I got down on the living room hardwood, or maybe it was boredom. I attempted to wedge myself under the coffee table but the space was too small so I gave up. I was so tired that every bone ached. I started to laugh at myself there on the floor, Kreeger down on the street under his bench. My body wrapped tight and warm, I stared into the black spaces under the furniture. I saw Delhi when I was five, and my mother – having returned for her father's funeral – dragging me by my elbow past the beggars in the night street. There were cities of them, the misery so close to me, the rancid smell of it like soured milk. My vision blurred the dust under the sofa into grey soft tumbleweeds, and I fell into a deep sleep.

Through the large windows, I see that the restaurant has a decent crowd but isn't full. I expect to have another fight with Kreeger over leaving his cart outside but he surprises me – and himself – I think, by pulling a bike lock out of one of his deep pockets. He drags the cart over to a streetlamp and wraps the lock around the post. Then, he weaves it through the tines, clicking it shut and dropping a small key in his pocket. I think I see him grin as I hold the door for him.

As I scout a table, he reaches up and wiggles his fingers between the red and green pepper-shaped lights that run up and down and around fixtures in the room. He really seems happy in this moment. Smells of braised beef and baked pastry come from a bright kitchen gleaming busy on the other side of a rectangular pass through window. A waitress, balancing a tray loaded with five main courses, tells us to sit anywhere we like. People turn and fix their eyes on Kreeger and then on me.

'Come on buddy.' I encourage him away from the hanging lights by putting my hand on his back.

'It's Christmas,' he yells. Spittle flicks my cheek, the remainder escaping down his chin. 'Pretty, pretty, Jesus lights.' He points at them individually and nods at the people who stare. It's as if he believes they all understand him and agree, as if he sees them all smiling back. They aren't.

I encourage my slow-moving friend into a booth with blue vinyl seats and one of those chrome-trimmed laminate tables from the 1950s. I make sure to choose a booth beside the window with its arc of gold-stencilled letters, so that Kreeger can see his parked cart outside. He runs his hands along the table edge, back and forth.

'Smooth,' he croons. He takes in the world as if he's an infant, every surface alive with information.'Smooth as silk. Smooth as water.' He's like a kid with a secret. Beyond his chapped lips, I see a black space where there should be a tooth, or teeth. 'As smooth as your mud-brown ass, buddy. Smooth.'

I smile at Kreeger's creativity. He's pegged one thing at least. Still, I don't want him commenting on any other multiethnic body parts so I shush him. I scan the room for colour, but it's predominantly filled with a blur of white faces. Bubbling behind it all, the hum of conversation and clinking of cutlery on plates, the clearing of throats, a soundtrack that takes me back to my high school cafeteria.

The first time I ever saw a fist fight up close was when a guy sitting at my table said, 'Go home rag head' to this puny grade nine who had just passed by, carrying his lunch. The kid stopped and the first thing we noticed was how skinny he was, his shoulder blades like giant thumbs holding up the number seven on the back of his orange soccer jersey, his turban an onion on his head. He turned and attacked like a wasp. His tiny fists grazed the white kid's face, buzzed his torso, his turban coming loose and unwinding like toilet paper. This brought an audience pooling into a tight circle. I was close enough to hear the kid's attempt at a sucker punch, eliciting nothing more than a sigh from the bigger guy. I couldn't stand the flesh on flesh smacks, the desperate grabbing. I knew number seven was doomed so I got up and was about to pull him off, but in the time it took for me to move around the long table, the kid had been knocked to the floor, his hands guarding his face, his knees up. He was an ant now, curled and defensive, and the big white guy was getting back up to finish it. I stepped between them and, as I offered a hand to the kid on the floor, felt the full on crack of some bone in my head.

'Shit. Get out of the way, man.' The big white guy

tried to get around me but I held steady waiting for the kid on the floor to take my hand.

He elbowed himself up and spat. Most of it missed me except for a warm phlegmy edge that connected with my outstretched fingers.

'Coconut,' he sneered at me as a teacher pulled him up and another grabbed the big white guy's arm and mine and hauled us to the office.

Two waitresses argue by the cash register, casting glances our way. The shorter one of the two – the top of her blonde head level with the other's shoulders – stops speaking a moment, her stubby arms crossed high on her chest. She glares at the floor then grabs two menus and waddles over to our table. She has bowed legs and has to move her whole upper body as she walks.

Kreeger follows my gaze. 'Midgets are people too,' he says.

'Keep your voice down.'

'My voice is down, Apollo. It's on the down low Apollo.'

He drums the table edge with two crooked fingers. He smells of street urine, and dirty unwashed body and rotten teeth. I'm anxious to get some sweet-smelling food delivered to cover up the stench.

The waitress hands us our menus. Kreeger lowers his rheumy lids to avoid her gaze. He stops drumming and fiddles with a loose thread off the corner of the menu binding. An '80s swing tune, Sea of Love, plays on a large jukebox in the middle of the room.

'Soup today is clam chowder. Our grand opening special is our Sloppy Joe over biscuits. That comes with your choice of vegetable and fries, potato or salad for $9.95'

She sounds bored. The only thing I can think is how tough it must be for her to get dates. She's not that old. Maybe in her early twenties but it's hard to tell even with pointers like her pierced eyebrow and her hyper rate of speech.

'Are you ready to order drinks yet?'

'What's on tap?' I ask and then realise, as she cracks a smile at my presumption, that the place probably doesn't come with a stocked bar.

'The finest city water, and you can't beat the price.'

'She has to be older than twenty-eight.'

'We aren't exactly licensed yet but if you're desperate–' She shoots a look at Kreeger. 'I think I might have seen a few Corona in the cooler.'

'You serious?'

'No.'

I sit back. I'm craving a beer, can taste it already, suds around my teeth, over my tongue. 'That great water you rave about will be fine for me. Kreeger? Coffee or something?'

The waitress scribbles then waits, which gives me time to read her nametag. Bonnie. I hate nametags. I hate labels. I hate names. Mine never served me well. Shameed. It was always misspelled, mispronounced. But in a weird way names are a big part of what I do – cataloguing names, birthdates, death dates, flags and arrows defining us – so I take care to get them right. Although I resent them for the presumptions they evoke, I respect that they carry with them a certain energy and power.

Kreeger won't look up and Bonnie rolls her eyes. He's gone back to stroking the chrome edge of the table with both hands now.

'Coffee and water should be good for both of us,' I say.

'You ready to order food yet?' She eyeballs my forsaken menu.

'Yeah, two of those tasty specials would be great.'

Bonnie turns her scrutiny on me, studies my face as she puts her note pad in her apron pocket. 'You live around here?' she asks.

I nod. 'Just up the road.'

'So, you know him?'

'Sort of.'

She looks at me without talking but she wants to, I can tell. Finally she sighs and collects our menus.

I look out the window. Someone has tied their dog to the pole that Kreeger's cart is locked against. The dog – its tail driven down between its legs – sniffs the bottom rung where the toe of a tattered running shoe pokes through a hole in a bag. I just want to go home now. The effort of deciding for Kreeger what he should drink and eat is too heavy for me. I don't want it. I don't need it. I could make up an excuse. I have to go now. I forgot that I have an appointment, that I'm meeting a friend, that I told my mother I'd visit her. Would he understand any of that? How long would it be before Bonnie tossed him on his keezer, even if I did leave him with a twenty?

Kreeger slumps further down on his bench and slowly falls sideways then rolls under the table.

'Hey buddy, come on, sit up.' I sound too familiar with him as if I'm his caregiver.

'Food,' Kreeger says from under the table, his voice muffled.'

'Yeah I know. I'm hungry too.' Kreeger doesn't respond but his breathing intensifies much too close to my knees. 'Damn it, Kreeger. Sit up or we'll get turfed. Look, they're watching us.'

Across the restaurant, in front of a large brightly-lit TV screen, Bonnie is a shadow, her head tilted back to look up to a man in a suit jacket and tie. Must be the manager. He acts casual but I can tell he's scanning the restaurant to locate our table.

'Watching, watching, watching,' Kreeger sings from under the table.

I give his leg a gentle prod with my foot to try to get him to move his bulky body out of the small space beneath the table and back up onto the bench.

'I'll show you how to fight, pansy ass.' He grabs my foot and holds on to it, trying to twist off my shoe. The laces are loose so it's easily done. Loud as a peacock, he squeals his victory. Heads turn from other tables and booths. Kids with spaghetti-smeared mouths, stare. Parents feeding babies in high chairs suspend spoons mid-air, which is enough to bring Mr. Manager over to see us.

'Problems?' He smiles at me past clouds of aftershave.

I smile back stiffly while trying to shake Kreeger off my leg. 'Man, I'm parched. Haven't even seen our drinks yet.' I raise an eyebrow.

'You know we have a policy–'

Kreeger's head appears first as he pushes himself up to sitting. He groans with the exertion and puts my sneaker on the table between us. 'Wild ride,' he grins at me and I see his rotten front teeth. His face is flushed making it seem as if his weathered skin may split. He puts a wad of gum from under the table in his mouth.

'Got finger bowls?' he asks Mr. Manager whose mouth gathers into a frown behind his moustache.

'Finger bowls? No. Washrooms are right over there.' He motions like a flight attendant, a little too vacant in the eyes, tight in the lips. He turns to me, appears to be weighing the stretch of time it would take to explain restaurant policy versus the simpler route of rushing us out the door. 'You'll have to keep it down,' is all he says. 'I'll go check on your drinks.'

'And cutlery,' Kreeger yells after him as he leaves.

I mouth the words, Shut up, and draw my hand across my neck, slicing my own throat.

'And napkins, the nice cloth ones. All the trimmins before we go over the falls.' Kreeger puts his hands in his lap and rocks back and forth. 'Elbows off the table, Winston Churchill, elbows off,' he says to me.

Bonnie moves back through the restaurant to our table balancing a tray of beverages. She visits another table first, puts a glass with rattling ice and dark soda in front of a man with red curls and a goatee. They share a joke as she puts a coffee mug in front of his companion. The woman thanks Bonnie, then slips on a coat trimmed with fake fur, stands up and walks out of the restaurant. Somehow, I know she belongs to the dog tied shivering beside Kreeger's cart. I don't know much about specific breeds but this one looks like some kind of poodle with a long pointy nose.

Outside, the woman's breath comes in faint puffs and she pulls her hood over tufts of white hair, protecting her head against the wet gloppy snow and leaving nothing much in profile but a high cliff of a nose and jutting cheekbones. She bends to untie and pick up the dog, and that's when Kreeger stops rocking in his seat and sits up tall to watch her.

He turns his wild eyes to me. 'Thief!' He points seemingly at a loss for what to do. 'Do something, Napolean.'

'Relax.' I put a hand over his fluttering pointer finger, think about the germ warfare writhing under his nails, wish for the finger bowls of his cultivated imaginings. 'She's just having a smoke break, and picking up her dog to warm him up.'

A strange look washes the tension from Kreeger's jaw, loosens the knit of his brows as if he's remembering some former time in his life, a happy time. Kreeger raps on the window. The woman holding the dog turns in response to the noise and Kreeger waves. Bonnie arrives and starts unloading our napkin-rolled cutlery, mugs of coffee, and perspiring glasses of water.

'The robber queen's got a warm little dog, midget woman,' Kreeger says to her.

Bonnie expels a long even breath that hisses from between her teeth. She files the empty tray under her short arm, flicks her eyes from the woman outside and back to Kreeger. 'You don't remember my name at all, do you?'

Kreeger grunts and tries to stand, using his hands as levers to push out of the booth.

'Hey buddy, what're you doing?' I ask.

'She's stealing my things! Out of my way, leprechaun. Move it,' he shouts at Bonnie at his full height now, but she won't budge.

She reaches up and rams my old soldier-friend in the stomach with her stubby index finger. It's probably

Kreeger's astonishment that topples him, knocking him back down into his trench.

'Bonnie, orders up!' a cook cries from the pass through window, a wide grin splitting his dark whiskered chin.

'In a minute,' she shouts. 'Listen.' She needles her stubby finger into Kreeger's chest. 'She's not stealing nothing. Who would want your crap anyway. She's having a smoke. Gotta admit I could use one right about now, too. You'd better behave yourself while you're here because there's no Uncle Bob to bail you out. And, don't call me Leprechaun. Those days are done.'

Kreeger looks as if he's going to cry.

'I'll be right back with your food,' she says.

The woman with the sinewy dog has put it back down on the sidewalk and it lifts its leg to take a leak on Kreeger's cart. I'm relieved that he hasn't looked up to see this latest trespass. I study my fingers and try to process everything I've just heard.

Bonnie delivers our Sloppy Joes. 'Two specials,' she mutters and I notice that now there are three cooks peering out the pass through window, looking at our table. Like a toddler playing with a spoon, Kreeger immediately mashes the hamburger meat and bun into as much a paste as possible. I think of my grandmother who, when she visited from India, used her roti as cutlery to mop up every last morsel of food at mealtimes.

Bonnie tries not to watch Kreeger mangle his meal by turning her attention to me. 'Hey, listen,' she says, 'I owe you an apology.'

I wonder if this apology has anything to do with

Mr. Manager's little lecture. I cross my arms and she carries on as if she's reciting a speech. 'Norman and I, we share a bit of a history,' she says softly.

'Norman?'

'Your friend, here. He was once, sort of a friend of mine, too.'

And this is how you treat friends, I think, but I decide to let her squirm. She's got it all wrong. This guy, my friend, is Kreeger, not Norman. He might look like every other guy out there on the street but he's smarter than all of them. He actually thinks about me through the day, otherwise why would he collect flyers? When I was still an archival intern I worked hard to decide on Kreeger's nickname. I was doing a research project on the Kreeger Coat of Arms. The old German word, Krieger, was once an occupational name for mercenary soldier. That was what Kreeger was: a warrior. Over time, he seemed to get used to his new name, accept it, respond to it.

'Any chance you might have the wrong guy?' I ask.

She shakes her head. 'Nope. Norm and I spent a lot of quality time together in detox.' After a pause she says, 'You can't fix everybody's problems you know.'

'Spare me,' I say and unroll my cutlery. 'Kreeger, use your fork.'

o0o

I think pie might be a nice finish to our feast; I choose the take-out option. I leave Kreeger at the table making pyramids of salt and pepper in a landscape of stained red crumpled napkins, while I go pay the bill.

Bonnie pulls out a stool behind the cash register. She hops up and I hand her my credit card. Instead of having to look up at me now, she looks me directly in the eye. 'You may not realise it, but he's got you pegged. You're the mark.'

'Yeah, like he's going to overpower me and rob me blind. Listen, I appreciate your concern. Somehow I didn't take you to be so–'

'Hard-edged? Paranoid? Blunt? Why, because I'm cute and little, and therefore harmless?' She hands back my card and frisks me with her icy blues, then motions to Kreeger bent over his miniature salt towers. 'And he's harmless because he's old, missing most of his teeth, and can't walk very well?'

On the receipt she slides over to me, I scribble .03 cents for 'Tip' and sign my name.

'I like you.' She smiles unconvincingly. Obviously, she hasn't seen the receipt yet. I panic a moment, think of changing it. 'But don't be fooled.' She tucks the credit card slip in the cash drawer.

'Well, I think he deserves a break. He's a decent guy. Probably just had a lot of bad luck.'

'See it the way you want. He's made certain choices. We all make choices. The guys in the kitchen are about one paycheque away from being him.'

With more than a little trepidation, I turn to see why she's looking at Kreeger. He's standing now, filling his deep pockets with the salt and pepper shakers, the used cutlery not yet cleared, all the napkins from the dispenser, even the restaurant's list of dessert specials in its little wooden stand.

As we leave the restaurant, Bonnie insists that Kreeger empty his pockets and he calls her a bitch. Thankfully, most of the other tables have cleared out before us. As I hold the door and prod Kreeger through, Bonnie says, 'I had an uncle. He was normal-sized and his favorite saying was, no good deed goes unpunished.' She rotates the Open/Closed sign on the door. 'Have a nice night,' she says and the chain rattles as we leave.

I think about choices on our walk back to the condo, and how they tangle us up in webs of obligation. For instance, how can I now say goodnight to Kreeger and leave him to his cold sleeping bag on the wet, snowy ground? Maybe Bonnie's right; I'm a fly being wrapped up, spun and wrapped.

Shivering in the cold outside the front door of the condo building, I invite Kreeger inside but remind him that he's not allowed to bring his cart and point through the glass to the sign on the far wall of the lobby that says, No Shopping Carts in Building. This doesn't appear to faze him.

The tug-o-war is brutal but he eventually wins, ramming the cart through the door, over my toes, into the foyer. I quickly survey the sidewalk behind us, the lobby in front of us, and see no-one. Kreeger squints in the orange light, his chest puffing with determination. He stamps his feet and shakes his body like a dog after a swim.

'Warm here, buddy,' he grins. 'Like soup.'

On the way to the elevator, the cart leaves muddy wheel tracks on the tiles behind it. We ride in the elevator, the cart wedged between us, beneath a second No Shopping Carts sign and I pray not to encounter another resident. The ding and bump of the opening doors startle Kreeger. After a considerable amount of time reassuring him that his cart is now safe inside my apartment, he agrees to be separated from it and we leave it in my front hallway. I ask him if he wants to sit in the kitchen to have his pie. He shakes his head unsure of what to do. I guide him to the sofa. He's trembling and his eyes are filling with tears. 'Are you going to call someone and send me off?'

'No, Kreeger. You can sleep here tonight.' I ignore the swell of panic. What about tomorrow and the day after that? Although the smell of the street on Kreeger has been slightly masked by fried foods and coffee, he still needs a bath. But, if I offer him that, then what? It's the weekend so no work tomorrow but what about Monday? What then? I look at my desk, the disarray of stacked books: Preserving Archives and Manuscripts; Guide to Environmental Protection of Collections; Canadian Council of Archives; a blizzard of loose papers, the blank computer screen, the deserted coffee mugs.

I imagine Kreeger beside the bathtub refusing to remove his sodden clothing, fighting me as I try to pull off his socks, groaning when I ask him to raise his arms above his head. I try to see myself as nursemaid lowering his skinny, naked, mysteriously marked body into the warm water, feeling shame and fear.

My face is hot so after I deliver our slices of pie out of their Styrofoam containers onto small chipped plates that I carry to the living room, I go to the sliding glass door and push it open. On the sofa, Kreeger curls the hem of his coat into his hands and kneads it with his fingers. He seems as vulnerable as a kindergartener on his first day in the big school, not sure how to navigate, what to say.

After we eat our pie, I tell Kreeger I'm really tired and put my oldest white sheets on the sofa, the ones that followed me from my parent's home and between which I hid so many things as a kid: frogs, ripped and stained jeans, stolen chocolate bars, the product of wet dreams, my second girlfriend quasi-naked.

Kreeger insists I open the balcony door so he can hear.

'Hear what?' I ask.

He doesn't answer, only watches me with sunken eyes, his neck sinking into his shoulders. He rocks back and forth perched like a wary bird on the edge of the sofa. 'You'll tire, Einstein,' he says.

After the lights are out, Kreeger says a litany of profanities, perhaps his nightly plea of protection from the monsters that lurk, but it doesn't take long for him to drift off. I hear him snoring while I stare at my bedroom ceiling. I thought sleep would come easily if Kreeger was here with me in a warm, dry, safe place. Instead, I can sense him close by and I'm in knots. Somehow, he's become this brittle thing with a pulse like string, ready to snap any minute.

Insomnia's worse when you have the responsibility to listen. I desperately invite sleep, pulling air deep into my lungs and I become hopeful, hearing the steady stream in and out, thick with the assurance of dreams. But it's not really sleep I fall into. It's a slight dip under, a faint flutter kick of my mind propelling me to a half-dream.

I push the lobby door open and search the front pavement for Kreeger. He's gone, leaving dirt and a few twigs in the spot where he usually sits. I lean on the stucco wall, rattle the collection of change in my pocket, then I place two golden coins – like the ones they place on Egyptian mummies – on the pavement beside the twigs.

'Hey, get away from there shit head!'

I turn but can't see him.

'I said get away!' Kreeger barrels from behind a hedge, his trench coat flapping like bat wings. 'Can't a man take a piss anymore? That's my spot.'

I stand and hold my hands up to show him I'm in agreement. 'Of course,' I say and gesture him back to his spot.

'Bloody moron,' Kreeger says, but he freezes when he sees the dollar coins glinting at him in the light from the condo building's lobby and foyer. He picks one up and puts it between his teeth. I can see dirt under his fingernails. The fabric from his fingerless gloves and his skin are the same matching grey. There's a fuzzy clunking noise that makes no sense.

I flinch myself fully awake, open my eyes. How long was I under? Was the noise part of my dream? Perhaps I'm so restless because my body misses the nightly ritual of standing on my balcony, watching the rest of the lights in the building switch off one by one, looking for Kreeger in the shadows of the street.

I get up. My bare soles navigate around edges of books and clothes on the cool hardwood. A quick inventory of the room shows me that Kreeger's cart has been rolled to a spot beside the couch, the silver grill like a toothy grin in the shadows. In the dim glow from the kitchen stove light, I see his abandoned boots on the floor, stinky, splayed and misshapen like insect corpses, but he's not on the couch. He's not in the living room. The sliding patio door is open wider than I'd left it and cold air bullies its way through the apartment.

Out on the balcony, Kreeger is wrapped in the white sheet cocooned into a corner. His chest rises and falls evenly, his breath white vapour, infiltrating the bleak chill. In his repose one of his unwashed hands reaches through the railing as if he's a prisoner longing for escape, for some way back to what he knows.

COMMENDED

GEORGE OLIVER

George Oliver is the pen name of George Kowalik, who is currently an English PhD candidate at King's College London. His research is at the intersection of postmodernism, contemporary Anglo-American fiction, and the New Sincerity. His thesis explores 'post-postmodernism' in the work of Jonathan Franzen, Zadie Smith and David Foster Wallace.

He is also a freelance film writer, with work published or upcoming in Bright Wall/Dark Room, Luma Quarterly, Off Screen, and Vague Visages. George has been writing short fiction since 2018 – recent publications include Lotus-eater, Quail Bell Magazine, Sweet Tree Review, and Tales from the Moonlit Path.

COMMENDED
OUEN PRESS
SHORT STORY COMPETITION 2019

NEWTHINK
by George Oliver

Breakdown as public spectacle. Bypassing any system of queue or vendor, choosing their own seats, they decorated the side of the street as I capitulated in the centre of it.

I fell apart in front of the audience, to great applause. I'm only what they're keeping bottled up. I'm a personal sum of the collective parts: unease, discomfort, agitation, angst. Ordinarily they bubble beneath the surface, only threatening release. I exploded the surface, scattering these parts across the road. I rambled about the end of the world, shouting at whoever would listen.

Later, in a more private setting. One of those moments I was alone but for my own thoughts.

In my head it was simple: I intended to kill him in order to become him. Somewhat. In my head there were parallels with Chapman and Lennon. I'd take his life and in some way add to my own, consuming a part of my Lennon surrogate: a conversely pathetic, insignificant creative mind, equally driven by the delusion that his "work" would save the human race. This was the job I had been given.

I too would take careful, meticulous steps to do it. Plan it over months, structure it around a series of encounters. There are no such obstacles as security or protection here, but I had to ensure that I enjoy the process. I need to. Otherwise what's the point.

o0o

She wakes up each morning wondering exactly how the world will end. She loses hours of her day listing the different alternatives in her head: exactly when, by whose hand, a result of which mistake, which ignorance, which oversight. She's a five-year-old going on fifty.

This anxiety cripples the Girl, day in and day out, as do those belonging to the "family" she's so often reminded she's a part of. The Father is desperate to cling onto the last modicum of stability in a world gone to pieces.

His anxiety requires a bit of context. It's all since NewThink, the government's illegalisation of public creative expression and abolishment of the industries relying on it: writing, music, film, theatre, television… the list goes on. The Father, a prolific and once successful novelist, had no choice but to carry on writing as part of the illegal underground network for the eight years separating then from now. Underground, the issues contemporaneous to the world pre-NewThink were still what everyone wanted to write and read about.

The Father couldn't relate to any of them. He is white, straight, male – justifiably, people don't want to hear from people like him at the moment. There are far more important things to talk about, and far more urgency that this conversation be heard now that the volume's been turned down and it's been relegated to below ground. Moralistically, the Father finds himself in the difficult position of recognising the need for a newer, more diverse palate of voices, but being unable to offer one himself. The powerlessness sickens him. He's also not a very good writer, but he needs to be able to put food on the table.

His son, the Boy, is crippled by an anxiety that could almost be context free and is applicable to many at his point in life: the anxiety of whether or not he suffers from anxiety. Almost two decades on the planet, he still barely knows the person he should be, even if he recognises the face in the mirror. His morning wakeup coincides with the same incongruity each day: "Is it all in my head?" He would die for the opportunity to spend twenty-four hours in his own company, able to see himself from the outside and realise that there's nothing noticeably wrong with him, be comforted by the knowledge that he looks fine.

The Mother's is the most straightforward of the four. The worry that something terrible will happen to her two children will attach itself to her, burrow deep into her head and refuse to leave it. The chance of this happening is statistically more likely than eight years ago, so she sees the danger in everything: quietness must mean something loud and dangerous is around the corner, good fortune must mean bad is imminent, niceness must be nasty in disguise, etc.

I became the involuntary fifth member of this family on a cold November morning almost two weeks ago.

I blew in with the wind and slotted into arrangement as if I'd always belonged there. My entrance was timely: I staggered in as the Father and the Boy were locked in conversation that had reached boiling point.

'… Stop trying to convince me that he isn't me! My friends agree; it's clear as fucking day. Why even bother calling him Hal… it's clearly me.'

'You know I'd never do that. I always separate my life from my work. Have to. '

'You've done it again. You've used your book to say what you haven't got the balls to say to me in person.'

'That's ridiculous.'

'I agree. A self-loathing teen too smart for his own good, second guessing his own therapy? The heroic parents there to save him? Do you think I'm stupid?'

'You've got it completely wrong. I know there are similarities, but he's not you.'

'I do know there's something wrong with me, you know. This is M.E. we're talking about. Writing about what's wrong isn't gonna make it right.'

I was watching people watch themselves. Tired of listening at the doorway, I planned to glide in, contribute something along the lines of "But then he'd have nothing to write about." A segue into joining this rich debate, this relationship-destroyer that I find perversely fascinating.

I only managed an inelegant stumble, followed by an attempt to clear my throat, which devolved into a coughing fit.

'Who are you? What are you doing here?'

I finished clearing my throat before I responded.

The Boy looked pleased that there's finally a new voice, a deflection from the Father's.

'I was just passing by. I'm not from round here. I've nowhere to stay and was wondering if I could stay the night. I have money.'

I was Joseph, a month early and without the pregnant Mary.

'We don't do that kind of thing. You could try further up the street, but it's unlikely.'

Since the world changed irrevocably those eight years ago, the archaic culture of welcoming in the weary traveller had not exactly seen a comeback. People were even more cautious these days. So, I tried a different approach.

'I couldn't help but overhear you. I love the Hal saga. Glad was my late-twenties bible. Adult Undergarment is seminal. I've read them all and I'm a big fan. Is there a new book on the way?'

'How did you know where I lived? People aren't supposed to know that.'

The worry was palpable. The safety of his family is an anxiety he shares with the Mother. Or, it's his own safety that worries him.

'I know people. Your kind of people. I'm a writer myself.'

The underground writing community survived entirely on internal trust. It was self-sustaining because it cautiously welcomed in new writers, no matter how dangerous this got as civilisation continued to crumble. The generations of writers pre-NewThink "made it" the same way I intended to; or so goes the story I was fabricating. They were unforgettably associated with or indebted to their contemporaries: Joyce and Beckett, Tolkien and Lewis, Eliot and Pound, Fitzgerald and Hemingway. Once canonised and now outlawed.

'Son, get our guest a drink.'

To me: 'Please, take a seat. You must be tired, wandering the street at this time of night.'

'You're very kind.'

The Boy returned with a scotch and placed it on the table in front of me.

'Thank you.'

'Where did you say you were from?'

I hadn't, so did. I then proceeded to feed the narcissistic writerly ego for the next two weeks. It didn't take long to win him over and gain his trust. I had successfully established the lie necessary to complete the task I'd been sent here to do.

o0o

I dream of fireworks tearing apart the sky and a plane crash of which I am pilot, killing hundreds. The idea, desirable compared with the reality I wake up to, ruins my day before it's allowed to begin. Here I'm one of the passengers.

The long winter hours pass with little progress as to why I'm here. I receive precisely zero further details to fill my notebook with: no more names of writers, publishers or editors; no new secret hideouts or meeting points; no additional threads to the narrative I have woven in the two weeks so far. A fantastical tale of brotherhood, painting the picture of this network of criminal activity, of active creative thought, of passionate originality, of dream making. All the things I have been trained to despise. A school of blasphemous thought. A melting pot of deception. Of artifice. The very things that destroyed the old world and must take responsibility for the division and polarity that characterise the new one.

FREE THINKING
EQUALS
DANGEROUS THINKING.

The mantra hardwired into my head for over a decade. Five words that go through my head on at least an hourly basis.

NewThink needed to happen long before it did. I'd not be here today, cleaning up the mess from the fallout. I'd not be out on this suicide mission, sustaining the lie that I'm a writer just like the Father. The one-man show is tiresome. And the fate I feared inexorable has already begun to systematically unfold, as predictable as if I were the character in a story: I'm becoming attached.

The most discernible point of attachment is between me and the Boy. This December afternoon I devote to observing him, allowing my notebook to spiral into distraction and irrelevance.

His resemblance to the Father is striking; or perhaps this is my brain giving the distraction an excuse. But it is.

The transition from childhood to adulthood is an entirely transformative one, passage between the only two disparate selves that are ever part of the life cycle. When you enter the latter, the former becomes a distant memory, a past life you might not forget yet can never reconcile. The situation in front of me is curious: it is as if the Boy's adult self has transgressed the rules of time and cheated its way into co-existing alongside himself during childhood. The Father symbolises the final image of what the Boy is experiencing in medias res: the wrong decisions, the missed opportunities, the wasted potential.

If adulthood is coming to terms with the fact that you are empirically alone, childhood is the progressive introduction of the idea. The Boy wears it on his sleeve: the terror of being prisoner of his own internal space, the resistance of this fate. He sees the ramifications of loneliness in his Father, he sees the cracks in the illusion of structure created by the job, the marriage, the children. And I can see him seeing it.

Mood is contagious, projected outward from the individual and onto the external landscape, where others collide with it whether they wanted to or not. I see the thoughts splattered out in front of him as he thinks them. The fixation on dying, without the active desire to die. The feeling of helplessness in the age of inaction. The position amongst a generation joining the adult world too late to be able to fix its problems.

I used to be passive too, someone who would combat injustice with something as inane as a piece of writing. You know, rather than actually doing something about it. I too would pretend my opinion had meaning and hide it behind innovation for convenience.

But then I found the NewThink Fighters (N.T.F.) I'd say I was coaxed into joining the movement, but it wouldn't be true. I chose it.

NewThink had been declared law and people were still ignoring it, not allowing the government to deliver on their promise. Broken democracy… people were thinking outside the box and getting it published. Disrupting the world as God wishes to see it by shooting it from an angle or in artificial light. Rejecting everything authentic about the way we live by paying actors to change their walk, or speak in accent, or wear a fucking wig. People were taking the precious sounds of the natural world and distorting them, adding effects, declaring the resulting product "art" as if it's a justification for how fake it all is.

It must stop. That's why I'm here.

The Girl enters my periphery, humming a nursery rhyme, interrupting my thinking. It almost makes me sad to think about how alone she'll feel within two more weeks. I'm going to take away everything she looks up to as she navigates the mess she was born into. She didn't ask for any of this. She doesn't commit the sins of her Father.

'I can hear you thinking', she declares on approach, precociously.

'So what am I thinking?' I beam, playing her game.

'You wish you were my Daddy instead of Daddy.'

Irrationally defensive, I respond: 'No I don't. You know, not everybody wants to be a Daddy.'

'But… why?'

'Some people have other things to do with the rest of their life.'

'But… why?'

Later that day, I find myself in the company of the Boy and the Girl.

'These stories are ours. They're private. He shouldn't be sharing all this with anyone but me.'

I scribble notes – nodding vaguely, willing him to go on.

'What's it like out there? What do people think of him? Who's reading this stuff?'

Realising I've been promoted to specific addressee, I fumble to return my notebook to my pocket before the Boy really notices it. There's nothing worse than knowing you're being written.

'Far more people than he thinks', I lie.

'Is he one of those writers now?'

'Meaning?'

'The ones that people begin to worship. The ones people can't leave alone. You know what happens to those kinds of people.'

'What happens to those kinds of people?'

'They fart and it causes a frenzy. They can't leave the house alone. They get no peace.'

'At least they feel wanted.'

The Boy sighs, but the bitterness is palpable. He'll never get over this. He'll never forgive the Father.

'Daddy loves you.'

I'm unsure if the Girl directs this at her brother, or if it's intended for nobody in particular. Merely a statement. A general, optimistic proclamation for a world that needs such things.

'... Daddy loves people who do the dishes when they're told.'

The Mother wears an unflinching expression that communicates "do what I say or risk getting on the wrong side of me". Her children may be at different stages of invincibility, but the outfit shakes me to the core. As they barely gratify her entrance with their attention, I step in.

'I can help with the dishes.'

She is unsurprised at this addition to my persistent offers of help around the house.

'Thank you, but you've done too much. You're a guest. We should be the ones looking after you.'

'I'm just happy to be here.'

'We're happy to have you.'

o0o

Two more weeks pass. My conclusions are scattered but coherent. Conclusive. I'd become less interested in the bigger picture and more invested in this family narrative: irreparable damage to a father-son relationship, an almost non-existent husband-wife one; patriarchal protection from the world around the family, but no protection from the patriarch himself. And most unforgivably: a general prioritisation of art over living.

The Father mines his own dissatisfaction for creative gain. Rather than try and fix anything, he presents the individual fragments of his life in a new arrangement, no more complete. Calls it "fiction". It's a sum of the conversations he doesn't have but should, the thoughts he keeps in rather than express, the artificial drama he could avoid or even resolve if he wasn't so fucking preoccupied by the idea of creating something.

His great mistake was not doing the same soul-destroying, meaningless work as the rest of us. Delivering the post, scanning barcodes, opening and closing a cash register, staring at a computer, watching the paint dry on the four walls of an office. This was his grand misfire. The career ender. The big-budget flop.

I experience these confirmatory, Final Act thoughts as I navigate the setting to this denouement: the family library, a space I've occupied on more than one occasion over these four weeks. The family library that exists solely to escape from the family. This is where the Father can be alone, where he can live. I walk in his footsteps, allowing my eyes to scan over the bookshelves, the names of the ghosts he idolises and will soon join: Ballard, Beckett, Borges, Bukowski, Burroughs… the rows and names go on and on and on, tediously "countercultural", self-importantly "boundary-pushing", predictably white male.

Variety and accessibility are entirely absent. The children's books gather dust in the furthest shelves most difficult to reach – neglected, rarely used, visual evidence of an untaken opportunity to give the Boy and the Girl a more normal upbringing under the circumstances. One even might be able to detect logic in. Rebellion against NewThink that would at least make a little sense.

The most damning evidence of how crazy this man is stared me in the face as soon as I entered, but I only notice it now: the section of his own titles. Paperbacks, hardbacks, first editions, reissues, signed copies, framed manuscript drafts. Everything imaginable, and then some. His own shrine. How utterly vain.

I scan the collection for any new notes to editors or messages from publishers, any form of indication of who exactly is sanctioning this, who is complicit.

I find everything. Enough ammunition to take down this circle. The first step of a complete takedown of what's left of the writing community. A grand-scale operation to wipe out every last one of them.

I'd achieved it in a different way than originally intended. When complete, my mission will have been one long encounter, rather than a series. I could've left and come back, presented my N.T.F. contact with findings periodically, rather than all in one go; but I didn't. It won't matter in the long run. Soon, I'll be able to sleep again.

o0o

On cue, the Father enters the library. Presumably to escape, as usual.

'Ahh… so you've found my not-so-secret hideout.'

I cut straight to it, diffusing any potential tension, disappointing my viewers at home – who, by this point feverish, reposition themselves at the edge of their seats for this Mexican standoff. Something is finally, actually happening:

'It's probably time I told you why I'm really here.'

'Umm, okay. Shoot.'

'I'm here to shoot you in the face.'

Predictably, he doesn't take this seriously. Smiles instead.

'I'm being serious.'

'This isn't funny.'

'It's not supposed to be. I'm tired of being funny. Do you know what else isn't funny? Politicians fighting over things that aren't even real. Stories, films, songs… a facsimile of living, instead of the real thing. Do you know what isn't funny? The children starving on the streets because of people like YOU, exhausting government funds and turning attention away from the compliant citizens of the world. Thanks to people like you, people like me are necessary.'

I'm shaking. The Father, meanwhile, is impossibly still. A statue of stupefaction.

'… I… I… I don't know what to say.'

'Well now's the chance. Say your piece. Have your moment. Everyone's waiting.'

'…'

'Why the self-mythology? Your stories – what's the point of them? The thinly veiled disguise of writing about somebody other than yourself isn't smart, it's gratuitous. You're not the first to do it.'

This time the Father's mouth moves and noises come out, not quite forming words. It's progress.

'There's something intensely annoying about your work. There's a reason I chose you, you know. They gave me a whole list and I chose you.'

'I feel so special.'

I'm impressed he's responded so soon into my diatribe; this wasn't how it played out in my head. Simultaneously impressed and excited, I step back and give him the floor for a short while.

'… Do you think I don't know that none of this matters?'

He grabs the nearest handful of books and throws them across the room. The drama is electrifying.

'I know it's all bullshit. Of course it is. It always has been. You know what though? Some of us have to do it. Some of us are no good at anything else. Who's supposed to provide for my family? Who's gonna put food in their mouths? Who's gonna make sure there's a roof over their head? This is my duty, man.'

The whole thing's exhilarating.

'I'm no good at anything else – this writing thing is all I've got. That's got to mean something. Some people deliver the post, some scan barcodes, some sit in an office; I'm just like them. It's nature. Otherwise, one day the world stops turning.'

'It already did', I point out.

'Exactly. I've been trying to fix it for the past eight years. What have you done?'

Internally, I give in. I've never been trying to "fix" anything. My mind answers "Relishing every second of the collapse. Adding kindling to the fire, grinning ear-to-ear like a Cheshire fucking cat"; but my mouth doesn't produce anything.

Instead, I offer a digression: 'Let's backtrack a second. That's nonsense – why is it only your prerogative? Your wife has something to give to the world too. You're not holding up the roof on your own. That kind of mindset is antiquated. You're gathering dust.'

'Don't go off script.'

'I'm not. It's not all about the Father – you're just self-entitled privilege, personified. Your conversation's stale. The counterculture is dead… have some goddamn sincerity.'

'Is this something your character would say?'

'What's that supposed to mean?'

'You hate people like me, the stories we tell, the worlds we create, the characters we make; but you're a character yourself.'

'No I'm not.'

'Yes you are.'

'No I'm not.'

'You are. I know you're not really a writer. I know who you work for – I can see through the N.T.F. rhetoric. I want to know your real name, not the fake one you've given me. I want to know what the real YOU thinks, not the hours of rehearsals. Not the pamphlets.'

'I–'

'You lot think you're a secret when you're not. The Resistance know everything.'

'I… I…'

'Come on man, you're stuttering. You've lost. I've got a Colt AR-15 semi-automatic hidden behind that bookshelf just there.'

He nods to the "K-O" section of his collection, beginning with Kafka and ending at Orwell. It's the one shelf I've never properly examined. Typical.

'It can do a lot more damage than the 9mm Glock G19 in your left shoe. Trust me, I've done the research. The AR-15 is unnecessarily powerful. But I've got to protect myself – the world's a dangerous place these days.'

He gives me plenty of time to process this information, generate my own thoughts, formulate a response, package, present. A goddamn eternity. It feels longer than the ten years of training.

Post-eternity, something peculiar happens. Right at the death, just as the curtain fall is imminent.

The Girl, humming the same nursery rhyme, enters the doorway of the library. Ordinarily, the Father would lock himself away here, but today isn't ordinary. The Girl takes full advantage of the lapse in concentration and newfound freedom, her eyes lighting up as she explores this entirely new world, full of playtime potential and toy stash possibilities.

The Father looks horrified. He's correct: he's won. But both he and I know that I haven't come all this way and done all this work to give up without a fight. So, he will have to use the AR-15. The Girl will see this and not be able to unsee it for the rest of her life. She won't realise the gravity of it until she's much older, screaming her way out the front door at eighteen, her parents and brother pleading with her to come back. To be rational. To not make a decision she'll regret.

She'll realise it when she's shivering under cardboard on a street corner, still homeless at twenty-four, nihilistically embracing a hopeless future in a world that's fucked beyond repair anyway.

She'll realise it at fifty-one, attending the funeral of a Father she'd forgotten, beside a Mother that doesn't remember her name.

She'll realise it at seventy-nine, dying in a hospital bed, with her first and last visitor at her side: her brother, determined to at least pretend to "forgive and forget" before they no longer can. She'll realise it then, when the pair can't get the words out nor see one another through the floods of tears of a lifetime, condensed into one cathartic five-minute conversation.

This, of course, being the projected narrative trajectory of only the likely outcome of what's playing out here in the present. My gift to the Father. It's been anything but predictable so far, so who knows, there could be a surprise in store. To reach the gift, you have to get past the wrapping paper.

No matter which way it goes, books will fly, shelves will topple, and the Father's library will be in a right state by the end of everything. It'll be a spectacle.

STEVE WADE

Steve Wade is an English language teacher, living in Dublin, Ireland. He says he was side-tracked by the demands of university studies, and then by the vagaries and demands of earning a living, before he could once more immerse himself in writing whilst living and working in Sardinia. It was a position that gave him the time and solitude to begin in earnest a commitment to writing short stories and novels.

Steve's award winning short fiction has been widely published and anthologised. He has had stories shortlisted for the Francis McManus Short Story Competition and for the Hennessy Award. His stories have appeared in over fifty print publications, including Fjords, Boyne Berries, Crannóg, Bridge House Publishing, New Fables, and Aesthetica Creative Works Annual. He has won First Prize in the Delvin Garradrimna Short Story Competition on four occasions. Winner of the Short Story category in the Write by the Sea writing competition 2019. First Prize winner in the Dun Laoghaire/Rathdown Short Story Competition 2020. He was a prize nominee for the PEN/O'Henry Award, and a prize nominee for the Pushcart Prize. He can be found online at *www.stephenwade.ie.*

COMMENDED
OUEN PRESS
SHORT STORY COMPETITION 2019

LAST REFUGE

by Steve Wade

His da's smiling face whispered down on him before Tommy was fully awake. Tommy heard the smile while his eyes were still closed.

'Rise and shine, Tommy. Happy birthday, son.'

Tommy smelled the smoky-brown smell mixed with after-shave. He loved that smell.

'Me birthday?' he said. 'Aw Da, I forgot.' His arms were around his da's neck hugging him the way he used to when his ma was still with them.'

'Here, son, this is from your ma and me.' He took a small, unwrapped box out from behind his back.

'Deadly, Da, thanks.'

It was exactly what Tommy wanted, a new smartphone. His da knew everything.

'Right, Tommy. Let's get ready. You and me is

going into town for some breakfast.'

'But Da, I thought you were in work today?'

His da straightened up and stood in front of the mirror in Tommy's wardrobe. He worked his splayed fingers through his hair and shifted his tie.

'Working?' he said. 'That's right. Another treat for you on your birthday.'

Confused about what his da meant, Tommy experienced a bubbling sense of anticipation in his stomach.

'It's Ma, isn't it da? Ma is going to be in town–'

'No, Tommy,' he interrupted. 'Your ma is gone. She won't be coming back never, okay?' His da's voice sounded angry.

Tommy suddenly felt like crying. But this was his tenth birthday. Ten year-olds weren't supposed to cry. He wasn't a crybaby.

'I'm sorry son,' his da said, sitting back down on Tommy's bed. This time his da was the one to wrap his arms around Tommy. 'I didn't mean to shout at you.'

He felt his da's body shaking a bit while he embraced him. He couldn't see his face. He heard him sniffle. His da must have been getting a cold.

Tommy's da left the room to feed the budgie and the rabbit. Tommy pulled on his white tracksuit, went into the bathroom and pretended to wash his face. He filled up the sink, read the time on his swatch watch, and then prised up the sink-stopper with his nails after two minutes – there was no chain attached. The water made a satisfactory gurgling-glug going down the plughole.

'What do you need your coat for, Da?' he asked

when he had squeezed by the rabbit hutch in the hall and half-skipped into the living room. 'It's scorching out. Look at it.' He pointed out the window.

The rusty-coloured facade of the block of flats opposite looked a happy coppery-yellow, and the burnt-out car he and his pals had grown tired of playing in weeks back drew him towards it like a frozen puddle. Later, when he and his da were back from town, he'd sit on the box they used as a driving-seat and listen to his new Smartphone.

'Presentation, son. You have to look the part. So, tell me, Tommy. How does your old man look?'

He undid the buttons on his trench coat, put one hand on the waistband of his slate-grey slacks, and struck up the cool pose he used when his photograph was being taken.

'Legend, Da. You're like the Men in Black.'

His da laughed his big laugh and said, 'Nice one, son. Now, come on, let's rumble, as the man says.'

The stairwell zigzagging down the seven flights to the ground had its familiar stale, dank, urinary hum, a smell that neither bothered nor offended father or son. They were accustomed to it. But the aftermath created by a late-night drinking session at the bottom of the stairwell had left a cloying, vomity stink in the trapped area.

'Bloody dirt-birds,' Tommy's da said. 'You know, they ought to put them Muppets down, the whole bloody lot. I'd do it meself if I had a gun.'

On the bus into town, Tommy watched the people from the upstairs window. They all appeared to be late for work or something. And he felt sorry for the kids going to school, especially those kids walking on their own. Their faces were sad. It wasn't their birthday, and they didn't have a cool da like his who let them have a day off school and who brought them into town and to his work.

In the city centre, they made their way into that street where there were no cars, only people. Tommy remembered being there with his ma and da. That was before the fighting and the screaming. He wished those memories would leave him alone on his birthday.

His da told him he had to have a word with a man, a buddy of his, who was standing outside a shop.

'You wait there and watch them young fellows playing guitars,' he said. 'And stay put. I'll be back in a minute.'

A small group of people quickly became a large wall of legs and backs. Tommy could no longer see the buskers. He remained where he was for a long time, because his da had told him not to move. But when he recognised the same song being sung by the band for the third time, he was worried that maybe his da couldn't find him.

'Da,' he shouted. 'Da, I'm here.'

He pushed his way through the crowd. Somebody shoved him. His da had disappeared from outside the shop. The man, his da's buddy, stood alone in the doorway. He wore black clothes. In a large pink fist, he clutched a walkie-talkie. His head was bald and Tommy didn't like his face.

'Are you alright, son?' he said.

Tommy realised he'd been staring at the man. In the flat complex where Tommy lived, there were a lot of what he and his pals called 'scumbags'. He'd learned not to look at these scumbags. His da called them 'Muppets'.

'I'm sound,' Tommy said. 'Thanks.' He moved off and concentrated on avoiding the bodies walking towards him.

A good bit down the street, he yelled out for his da again. He heard his own voice sounding like a crybaby's, but he kept shouting, even though it hurt his throat.

He ignored a few people who asked him if he was lost. Some of them shouted after him. Their voices were nice, the way aunties and uncles sounded on TV.

'Hang on there, scobie,' a tall policeman said. He'd come from behind Tommy and clamped a hand on his wrist.

'I didn't do nothing,' Tommy said. 'Let us alone.'

The more Tommy struggled to free himself from the policeman, the tighter he gripped Tommy's arm. He jerked Tommy back by the scruff of his tracksuit top. Tommy heard something rip.

'You just relax, scobie,' he said. 'Come over here and let me talk to you.' He dragged Tommy across to a shop-front.

'I want me da,' Tommy said.

'What's your name?' the policeman said, using his free hand to slip a notebook and pen from his shirt-pocket.

'Da, help us,' Tommy roared. 'Where are you, Da?' he continued to shout in between convulsive crying.

'Excuse me, guard,' a man's voice said. 'What has this boy done?'

Still clutching Tommy by the wrist, the guard twisted sideways and around. The man, who wore glasses and had a red beard, stepped forward and stood next to Tommy.

'I suggest you move away, sir, and don't interfere with the law,' the policeman said.

'Bullies,' the man said. 'Too many of you people have an unhealthy attitude towards minors.' He produced a wallet from his inside pocket, removed from it a card and held it up to the policeman's face. 'I am the law,' he added, and used some big words Tommy didn't understand.

The tall policeman seemed to shrink. He extended his hand to the bearded man and, in a voice that might have been unsure whether it was supposed to be laughing or serious, said, 'Garda Brian Doolan, your Honour.' His wide smile put Tommy in mind of Shrek.

Tommy stepped backwards, not yet realising he was no longer being restrained by the policeman's huge meaty hand.

'You have ten seconds,' the bearded man said, 'ten seconds to give me an explanation as to why this boy is in such a distressed condition.'

'But, your Honour–'

'Seven,' the man said.

'They're all the same,' the policeman said, and drew his flabby hand across his forehead. His armpit was saturated. A darker patch of blue than the rest of his shirt clung beneath his arm.

'Ah,' the bearded man said. 'So you have taken it upon yourself to not alone police the streets, but to act also as judge and jury?'

Tommy became aware of the crowd of curious faces gathering around. A few faces were laughing, others goaded. It was like being trapped in a circle of boys in the schoolyard forcing you to fight another boy when you didn't want to. Scrap Scrap. Scrap.

'He's been up to something,' the policeman said. 'I know his father. Saw the two of them earlier up the street.' He frowned briefly at Tommy. 'Look at him!'

Tommy shifted his eyes onto the man with the beard. The man continued to somehow stare down on the far taller one. A strange laugh fell from his unsmiling beard. Normal-sounding laughter rippled through the curious crowd.

'Prejudice,' he said. 'You would do well, Garda Doolin, to look up this word in a dictionary.'

'Please, your Honour. I have to patrol this area … protect the people.'

His eyes, hooded by heavy lids, swung at the gathered crowd.

'Protect the people? And who, my friend, can the people rely on to protect them from pre-judgement and Gardaí who resort to less than circumstantial evidence to harass the public for acts of criminality that have yet to be established?'

The policeman apologised to the bearded man. The bearded man made him shake Tommy's hand and say he was sorry. Tommy thought it was some kind of a trick, but no handcuffs were placed on his wrists.

The bearded man asked Tommy if he was okay, once the policeman had moved hurriedly down a side street. Tommy felt like crying again. He wasn't used to strangers being nice to him. He told the man exactly what had happened. The bearded man gave him a ten-euro note for his birthday. One euro for every year, he said. He then walked him back to the shop where his da's friend watched the street through scumbag eyes.

The scumbag took his hands out of his pockets, listened to the bearded man and nodded his head a lot. The scumbag called him 'sir', and agreed that there wasn't any problem. 'No problem. No problem,' he said a number of times. He could do that right away. Yes sir. He even stuck an 'ohe' onto 'problem' once or twice – 'No problemo,' he said, in case the man wasn't convinced.

Before he left, the bearded man shook the scumbag's hand, ruffled Tommy's hair and hoped he'd have a great birthday.

The scumbag tore a mobile phone from out of his combats, flipped it open and stabbed a few buttons.

'Hello, Wacker,' the scumbag said into the phone. His sneaky eyes listened and his baldhead bobbed. 'I know what you mean. … Right. … I got you. But, listen, Wacker. You're not going to believe who came up to me on the door. … What? … No, not your man … Just get here, right. Your young fellow is waiting here for you in anyway. … Who? … Right, Tommy. That's his name. Okay. I have you.'

While they waited for Tommy's da to come back, the scumbag banged-on about football and some referee or linesman whose neck he'd take pleasure in snapping. He'd do time for it. No sweat. Copying the scumbag's head movements and expression, Tommy nodded and frowned. He wondered if his da was going to turn up with his ma after all.

'Here's Wacker now,' the scumbag said. 'I mean your old man.'

'I thought I told you to not move?' his da said when still only in shouting distance from Tommy. He walked up to Tommy, leaned down to him and rested his hands on Tommy's shoulders. He repeated what he had shouted. His words were dragged out and there was that nasally twang in his voice that Tommy hated. Tommy smelled the ugly sourness coming from his mouth. He'd had a few scoops.

Tommy's da told the scumbag that your man wasn't there, but they'd maybe hook up later, the three of them, in the boozer. That was game-ball with the scumbag. He reminded Tommy's da that it was his young fellow's birthday and that he'd let them go.

Tommy wanted to hold his da's hand as they walked through the street. He didn't. If his ma were with them, she'd hold his hand. If she came back now, Tommy would hold onto her hand forever. He'd never let her go.

A blast of heat clouted Tommy in the face when they stepped into the cafe. There was a hungry smell in the warmed-air. The same smell that crept up the stairs in his gran's house on Sunday mornings when he slept over on Saturday nights – the smell of sausages and rashers sizzling on a frying pan. The clink and clank made by cutlery on plates gave him a thrilling feeling, like listening to Eminem or 2Pac. The same feeling, yet somehow different.

The large cafe, which was self-service, his da said, was divided into different-sized sections. They could have been in a house with lots of rooms, and the people in the rooms might have been families having their breakfast at separate tables.

'This'll do us lovely,' his da said. He hung his trench coat over the back of a chair and told Tommy to sit in one of the three other chairs while he went to fetch the grub.

Tommy recognised, at a table near the stairs, two of the big boys who'd been playing music in the street. One of them had pink hair like a girl. Leaning against the wall and on a chair were their guitars in cases. He decided that he would play a guitar when he was bigger. Maybe his da might give him a guitar for his next birthday. But he'd never ever, no way, change his hair to pink.

'Right,' his da said. 'Here we are. A big breakfast for a big lad on his birthday.' He placed a plate in front of Tommy. On it was more food than Tommy had thought you could put on a single plate. 'Get that into you, son.'

Tommy would have preferred a burger and chips in McDonald's, but his da told him to eat what he was able to and leave the rest. It didn't matter.

Tommy decided he'd eat the sausages, have a go at the rashers, but wouldn't touch the egg.

They ate in silence. Tommy was used to his da not speaking at the table, and was surprised when he whispered across the table a comment about the blonde girl clearing the tables. 'A little smasher, isn't she?' he said.

This embarrassed Tommy. He dropped his eyes onto his plate and concentrated on removing the stringy fatty stuff from a rasher.

'Sorry, love,' his da said to the blonde girl as she moved next to their table.

'Yes, sir?' the girl said. She talked funny.

'I found this thing in me scrambled egg,' his da said. He showed her a hair-clip covered in scrambled egg – like one of the ones belonging to Tommy's ma that was lying around at home.

The girl's pretty face screwed up. 'I don't know,' she said. Her face wore a crooked smile.

Tommy's da twirled the clip between his fingers. Bits of egg jumped from it. The girl shifted backwards. His da then stabbed the clip into the remaining scrambled egg on his plate. 'The manager,' he said. 'I want a word with the manager.'

The girl's crooked smile collapsed. She indicated that she didn't understand.

'Jesus,' he roared in the voice Tommy hated. 'The manager. The manager.'

'I'm the manager, sir,' a small man in a dark crumpled jacket said. 'What's the problem here?'

'I found this in me breakfast,' his da said. He dug out the clip, speared a piece of egg with it and showed it to the small man. 'Only I had me head down, looking like, at me plate, I would've swallowed it.'

The small man took the clip from Tommy's da, shook off the piece of egg, and examined it as though he'd never seen a woman's hair-clip in his life. His cheeks were red, and Tommy thought his face was about to cry. 'It's very unusual,' he said. 'Do you have your receipt?'

The unhappy little man went away with the receipt and returned with some money, which he gave to Tommy's da. By his side was the blonde girl. She looked frightened. She placed a mug of coffee and a glass of coke on the table. The manager switched them, the coke for Tommy and the coffee for his da.

'The refreshments are on the house, sir,' he said. 'And the management apologises unreservedly for the other inconvenience.'

'Not a bother,' Tommy's da said. He fumbled through the notes and change given him by the little man, plucked out a few coins and addressed the blonde girl. 'Here love, this is for you.'

The girl hesitated, looked at the manager – he nodded consent – before reaching out and receiving the coins, about three euro Tommy reckoned.

'That was real nice of you, Da,' he said when the girl and the manager were sucked back into the cafe's heat and din.

'Nice to be nice, Tommy,' he said. He raised the notes given him by the manager to his face, kissed them, and shoved them into his shirt pocket.

Tommy felt bored with the cafe now. He wondered about going to his da's work and asked him.

'This is me work, son,' he said.

'You work in a cafe, Da?'

His da told him, as he always told him, that he did a bit of this and that. Confining himself to the one job wasn't where it was at.

Tommy didn't get it. He didn't want to get it. The way his da shifted about in his seat, fixing the coat on the back of his chair, yawning, stretching, and pretending to laugh at nothing clawed at him like a shameful memory of something that never happened. He tried to steer their conversation in another direction.

'Tell us about Lizzy, Da.'

His da's eyes locked onto Tommy's. His left arm shot upwards and away from him, clutching the imaginary neck of a guitar.

'The boys are back in town. The boys are back in town,' he sang, and his fingers danced along an invisible fret-board. 'Thin Lizzy,' he said. 'Best band ever. Good old Philo on bass and vocals.'

'Da,' Tommy said. 'Da, behind you.'

'What? What is it, son?' He craned his head sideways. 'Sorry boss,' he said to the stout man whose seatback pressed against the back of his da's chair.

'Your jacket's on the floor, boss. I must've knocked it down.' He reached behind him and swiped the man's coat from the ground and made a mess of attempting to put it back on his chair.

The stout man thanked him very much. He spoke and kind of laughed at the same time. His voice was full of air.

'Can we go now, Da?' Tommy said.

'We're going,' his da said. 'Just give us a few minutes, son, to pick meself up.'

'I need to go to the toilet, Da.'

'Tell you what, son. Let's move to them seats over there where there's more room and the whole lot. You can barrel-off to the jacks and I'll wait for you, alright?'

Something like panic gripped Tommy. What if his da was gone when he came back? Maybe his da was planning on running away with Tommy's ma. He'd never see them again. He'd be alone forever.

'I'm not too bad,' Tommy said. 'It'll wait.'

He followed his da around the small, tightly packed tables. They seated themselves at an empty, though cluttered, table over-looking the ground floor. The old woman Tommy's da asked to push back a 'teenchy bit' scowled at him before shifting her chair forward. Her face was full of thin stripes, like his gran's face. She muttered something to her husband.

Afraid that his da might break into another song,

Tommy commented on the people they could see sitting at the tables on the lower floor.

'Look at that family, Da. They're so fat. The ma is as big as a hippo. And the da is like your man on the telly, you know that funny guy?'

'What about the kids?' his da said. 'Two rolly pollies.'

Tommy laughed because his da laughed. Being fat wasn't funny, he knew, but hearing his da chortle made him happy.

'Why do people read books, Da?' he asked, noting a red-haired man with very white skin whose eyes were locked to a book propped against a bowl or something. Even when he drank from his mug, the red-hair continued to read.

His da took a slurp from his coffee. 'The same reason they go to school,' his da said. 'To learn things.'

'You mean like maths and Irish, Da?'

'Not exactly, son. Books helps you get smarter.'

'Da, you're smart, and you don't read books.'

His da bunched up his face. His eyes creased. 'A different kind of smart. Books helps you get a better job. When you're starting out in life and the whole lot.'

'What type of jobs is good jobs, Da?'

'His da's mouth did its turned-down it depends expression. 'Working for yourself is a good job, for example. You're your own boss.'

'Is a teacher a good job, Da?'

His da seemed to consider this for a while, or maybe he wasn't listening properly. He was busy shuffling around in the lining of his coat hanging on the back of the chair again, and wasn't getting beyond a few words.

'A teacher?' he repeated. 'A teacher, a good job? Is that what you're saying, Tommy? A teacher?'

'Do you know what I'd like to be when I grow up, Da?'

His da removed the overcoat from the chair and folded it in his lap. At home he usually left his coat wherever it landed. 'What's that son, a rock star?'

'I want to be Spiderman.'

Everything happened so quickly then. It was like playing a computer game. Tommy felt a part of the action but outside the screen at the same time. He never did get to tell his da what he'd do if he were Spiderman. He'd stop mas and das from shouting at each other and smashing stuff in the house when they were drunk. And any policeman that was bad with young fellows he'd wrap up in a web and pull them to the top of that big spiky-thing in the centre of town.

'Come on, Tommy, We're going.'

His da was already manoeuvring around the tables for the stairs.

'That's him, guard,' Tommy heard a man's voice saying. 'I've had my eye on him since he came into the shop.'

Tommy froze. When he thought back on the day of his tenth birthday over the years, he would recall more sharply than anything else the image of the huge policeman climbing the top steps that led into what would turn out to be his da's last refuge. The policeman's presence in the cafe was wrong. The way a butcher in his white and bloody coat walking up the aisle of a church might be wrong.

The stupid Shrek-smile on the policeman's face had been replaced by an expression that was both dangerous and frightened.

'Randal McCarthy,' the policeman said. Tommy had almost forgotten his da's real name. For Tommy, his da was 'Wacker'.

'He has that man's wallet,' the skinny floor-security man said, indicating the stout man whose jacket his da had earlier replaced on the man's chair.

Tommy glanced at the stout man. His face, smile-emptied, wore yet a shadow of a smile. The man looked at Tommy. He seemed embarrassed. He patted the outside of his jacket the way adults did when they were searching for something.

'My purse. My purse,' the stripy-faced old woman said. 'Oh, my God. He must have my purse, too.'

'Come on, Tommy, move,' his da said, but, the thing is, his da remained where he stood.

'Don't make me do it, Wacker,' the policeman said. 'There's nowhere to go.' In a shaking hand he tapped a black truncheon on his palm.

'That's right,' said the security man over the policeman's shoulder. 'You're nicked.' He looked more like an older boy than a man.

From Tommy's da came a roar, a bellow that a trapped animal in a programme on the telly might make. The stout man had Tommy's da's arms locked to his sides. His flabby arms had fastened around his da from the rear.

'Get off me,' his da screamed. 'I'll burn down your fuckin' gaff.'

When the handcuffs were slapped onto his da's wrists and he no longer struggled as he lay facedown on the floor, the policeman got up from his knees. He turned to Tommy. He seemed to see him for the first time.

'I knew you were up to something, the pair of you,' he said. 'You lot never change.'

Tommy prayed in his head that none of this was real, that it wasn't his birthday, and he was in his gran's dreaming on Saturday night, that his ma had never left, and that he had already gone to the toilet in the bathroom.

ANDREW SELLORS

Andrew has worked as a farmer, factory worker, painter and postman as well as studying four nights a week for four years to gain his Law degree. He uses these experiences and the people he met during them to form a rich palette of rough, working characters and clasping plots in his fiction.

As well as drawing upon his colourful life, his writing work is inspired by the styles and voices from his own voracious reading, which opts for the unpredictability of the country road rather than the speed and monotony of the motorway. Veering between James Joyce and Marie Kondo and from drama to prose to poetry, these influences instigate in him what pulls somebody into your work and what holds them there. Through creating this magnetic fiction his writing lifts the covers on a sly, sullied world of shifting characters none of whom can be trusted.

Andrew is a new, distinctive voice who has no limitations or boundaries and aims to push a reader off in a new direction. He believes it important not to just consume culture, but to create it for others too and that is why he writes.

Andrew lives in Derbyshire with his wife, who he says will not let him wear dungarees!

COMMENDED
OUEN PRESS
SHORT STORY COMPETITION 2019

CAUSA MORTIS
by Andrew Sellors

Come, pull up a chair and sit. The metal one with the blue padding is fine, bring it a bit close but not so close I can feel your stinking breath on me. Sit back, relax. Don't be nervous. Nobody is watching us for we are alone. Or at least we should be. Drink? Fine, but I will need one. My name? You can call me anything you want, I don't care. All I ask is that you drop your guard and open your mind but not too much though, as you can still never be too careful or trusting in these times. What I'm going to tell you is part truth, part lies. Which part is which I will leave you to decide.

In those days I considered myself to be a member of a very old and wise profession, not that you would ever have wanted to meet a member of my profession at work, for we were men of the night. Borrowing its black cloak to numb and manipulate your senses to our presence, burrowing into and hijacking your lives so we could exploit you for our own ends. Like silhouettes of a nightmare the darkness belonged to us. You were unlikely to hear us. You were unlikely to see us.

It was during one of these evenings that I was returning from my work. It had been one those nights when the cold penetrates down to your very bones. The freezing wind slaps against your exposed cheeks smacking them with a red kiss. Your mind seems to have lost control of your numb fingers and toes, which only move only as remote protrusions through the pain that has been instilled in them. The tortuous cold was somewhat alleviated by the weak pump of warmth from my van heater, even so I still bore hat, scarf and fingerless gloves.

I like driving at night. The swift unobstructed progress, the sweet luminescent aura of glowing dials for company as your mind railroads you home. For in the night this never-ending ribbon of tarmac is yours, just yours.

Occasionally though someone or something will rudely interrupt your automotive ponderings. Normally it's a bandity fox skipping across the road or drunks waivering around on pavements like wobble toys. They never usually bother me, I go my way and they go theirs. I don't appreciate company; anybody who says they are my friend is a liar. Anyway, this one evening I'm in the van, chugging along down some back street, minding my own business, some scatty little pop song on the radio. I'm feeling good and I'm thinking ahead to getting home and having back into the warmth.

Now, it's funny what goes through your mind when it happens. Even though it must last about a second, the mind seems to be able to stretch it out into a full-blown melodrama and one that is nonsense at that. What went through my mind in those seconds was this: funny time for a kid to be out on its own. Then I cut off. I can't remember the impact, I can't remember any noise. Maybe I had my eyes closed for me. *You don't want to see this.* I came to a halt in the middle of the road. Then it kicked in: I had hit something. *It was a fox* flashed across my mind. *Just a stupid fox, let's get out of here.* The engine was still running. *Put her in first and off you go.* No, I couldn't do that. What if on the off chance it had been a drunk? Or worse a kid? There would be consequences. What if there were witnesses? You can't just scurry away. I needed to get out and check what it had been. *It'll be a fox or a dog.*

I undid my seatbelt and opened the van door. I swung around on my seat so my legs hung out across the sill. *Just catch your breath.* I took in a gulp of air and rose. One thing that the night trains you in is silence. Till you have sampled the dearth of night you don't realise how soaked we are in noise during the daytime. Blood pumped around my skull as I walked down the side of the van. The pit of my stomach fell. It wasn't a dog or a fox. It was a person. *This is serious* I thought. I put my palms on my forehead and placed both elbows on the side of the bonnet. *What if they are dead?* Loot in the back and a dead body? They would throw the book at me. Wait – they might still be alive. Maybe I could drag them to the side of the road; leave. Somebody would pop along shortly. They wouldn't remember what happened. It wasn't ethical but they would survive. *I* would survive more importantly. *Check their pulse.* I hunkered down next to the body. It was tall, with brown curly hair. A man, yeah it was man. A drip of ruby-red blood ran from the corner of his mouth, down his cheek and onto the tarmac. Then I looked at the rest of him, sprayed across the tarmac. I was taken aback. He was wearing shiny, black overalls that were made of the kind of plastic you would get on a thick dustbin bag. On his feet he had a pair of grey, clog-like shoes, the kind of footwear that a nurse or a cook might wear. *It must be fancy dress* I thought, then I dismissed the idea, after all fancy dress as what? I placed my forefinger next to his throat hunting for the undulation of a pulsing artery. His youthful, pale skin was taut but cold. That was not a good sign. No pulse, no life, nothing. I checked the other side of his throat. Nothing. He was gone.

Now, I've killed before: man and beast. Looked into the whites of eyes just before the pull of a trigger or the plunge of a knife. Do you know what courses through your head just before you pull that moment? Of course you don't, you're just a little welt. Well, when you do take your first what will go through your mind is that you are at the briefest of moments the ultimate abuser of power and control, after all you are telling them to die and that's what they are doing. For a brief instant it's such a rush, you know then why serial killers do what they do. That day though? Nothing. Nothing like that. Maybe it was because I hadn't chosen to create an ending, it had been chosen for me. I felt panicky and panic is your worst enemy, it makes you rush your cognition and that's how mistakes are made.

So panicking, I got hold of his collar and dragged him up onto the pavement. Sprawled out he looked like a dozy drunk, rather than a piece of road kill. I took a deep breath, turned and got back in the van. I knocked the van into gear and hit the accelerator all the way back to the flat. Once back home I locked the door and sat with my back to it. *Nobody saw you.* Well, not that I know. My emotions buckled and I cried breath-sucking sobs. *Stop.* I had to stop this, crying wouldn't change a thing. Business had to go on as usual. There was work to be done. My mind needed something to deflect it from the idiot who had found his end on the bonnet on my van. *He was probably drunk, got what he deserved.* I needed to get back to work so I unzipped my coat before reaching for my small blue bag which, during work hours, resided in a deep, chest height interior pocket. The bag was about ten inches by ten inches, with a surface of smooth crumpled velvet that flicked between two shades of blue depending upon the direction it was combed in. Its neck garrotted by a length of black cord. I lay the exposed bag in my palm, taking in its weight I bounced the bag up and down, like a seductive dumbbell.

I filched it all during those years. And you know what? I can remember every single piece. Tiny hoops of silver ring, their shanks worn blotchy from dowager's fingers; great strings of cream-coloured pearls that would have bent and flowed with the contours of a wispy neck; heaving blue onyx rings like the eye of some hideous monster.

I walked into my sitting room where I pulled up a chair and placed the bag on a table. The cord of the bag released I placed my hand into the dark hollow and plucked out my items one by one. A small diamond, with a multitude of squared off surfaces that even off cheap light glimmered, a couple of dangly earrings with long golden tails and an amber pendant which had a luscious filthiness to its stone. That was not it though.

What was that? A noise? What noise? I didn't hear anything. From where? It's probably just the plumbing or something. You youngsters are so nervous these days. Don't get up, sit down! You hear! Stop it, get a grip. Here, have a sip of this to calm you down, you look pale. Oh, suit yourself. Right, where I was?

At this point I was spending time on the pretty and valuable facets of my haul. The golden rule of my profession is that you turn over your stock quickly. In out, shake it all about. I was quantifying what I did have and fixing in mind how many tokens I expected it to fetch the following day. The earrings, a nice fifty. They would look lovely on a fine woman. That pendant? Hundred? Hundred and fifty? That would be for the discernable crowd, someone a bit more discreet. Plenty but not going to shout about it. Now, that diamond. That really was exquisite; I hadn't seen something this tasty for a very long time. Mounted on a delicate gold ring it would seduce the senses of would be suitors.

Now, there is something about your face I don't trust, your eyes. It's your eyes. Put it down! Put it down! Calm it. No need to take it like that. Have it easy. No point getting your tail in a spin. We are all on edge these days and I'm no different. You could be one of them for all I know. I'm just too stupid or old to believe you aren't. Get me another drink. Whooaah! That's enough. Thanks. We've come this far, so we might as well finish.

It wouldn't do. Even though I was sat with some very beautiful and valuable items I still couldn't shift him from my brain. If he was a drunk then why hadn't I smelt drink on him? And those clothes? If he was a workman it was pretty funny gear to be working in. A lot of my answers would come from the news tomorrow; he was bound to crop up. Name. Age. Profession. A crying relative appealing for information. I would have to bear that. *Do not cave in, whatever you do.* No, I couldn't give in and go spilling all to the Noseys. Better to sit here and cry about it than sit and cry about in some cell, because that's where I would end up. Hopefully he wouldn't have kids, oh no not kids. It's one thing to kill a man out, but a father – now that was a enough ammunition to take the evasive out.

What's matter? Cat got your tongue as they used to say. If I'm boring you be on your way. Go. Leave. Oh that's right, but you can't can you. I forgot. You can't put me down; you want to know how it finishes, what's the twist in the tail? Plus you know too much now. You couldn't face Them, you would piss yourself after five minutes. Let out everything I told you. Not that it would bother me. The truth means nothing to me. I mean nothing to you. However, I'm not the one who is afraid. I've crushed my enemies, buried my friends. There is nothing left they can use against me, nothing could make me blab. I welcome death. Alright, no need to be petulant with me, I'm being nice to you.

Easy kid! Easy! Oh... you've bloody spilt it. No, leave it. I said leave it! Bloody kids, can't hold a drink metaphorically or literally. Anyway, sod that we need to continue.

Then it comes. A noise. My blood runs like ice and I solidify on the spot where I'm stood. A man of my profession does not appreciate unsolicited noises. *Ignore it, it will go away.* I shut my eyes as if that was some previously undiscovered way of cutting out the noise. It came again. *Go away.* My mind fuzzy I struggled to comprehend what it was. It came again. I had to kick into gear. Engaged with the world again I deciphered it: it was a knock at the door. That was bad news. Stolen goods, a dead body. *Prognosis: bad.* I had to get a grip because how I handled the next few minutes would determine whether the next few years of my life were in this flat or in a prison cell. I was determined it would be the former.

Think. Right the jewellery. The earrings, diamond and amber pendant were loud and proud on display. I grabbed them in a crude handful and tossed them out of the window. Hopefully if I could deal with the Noseys a quick post tet-a-tet retrieval from the bushes would have them back in my possession. The haul drifted down through the evening sky and into the oblivion of foliage down there. Another knock came. They were getting impatient out there. *Ok, let's be methodical here. The jewellery: dealt with.* Now, I had to exonerate myself of any hint that I had killed a man earlier. I moved over to a mirror and looked at myself. Shirt unbuttoned. *Button it.* Hair a bit sticky out. *Grab that comb.* Nervous. *Deep breath.* Right, I was as ready as I ever could be.

Briskly I strode over to the door and undid the catch. *Confidence.* I was going to be in control of this encounter and that would obvious to my visitor from the first moment. I would dictate what happened over the course of coming events.

'Good evening, how can I help you?' I said self-assuredly.

The visitor was not wearing a long blue coat or any silver buttons. So not a Nosey then. Instead this visitor was a very tall, willowy red headed female with a freckly face and large blue eyes. She wore a long, egg yolk coloured raincoat under which was a pair of blue jeans that wrapped around her thin legs, the ends of these disappeared into a pair of blue wellington boots which made her feet look clumsy. She didn't look like a professional officer of the law, and that was a relief. The professionals can smell a liar at forty yards, that's what they are trained to do after all. *Don't be deceived here.* A sudden gate of caution dropped down. Ok, so she didn't look like a Nosey. She wasn't dressed like a Nosey, but appearance can be deceptive. What if this was a rouse and she was? *Be on your guard fella.*

'Sorry to disturb you', her accent was strange – like a mixture of French and American syllables that competed with each other. 'But *I* need to see you'. *She's not a nosey.* This could be his sister or wife. The gates of thought suddenly banged into locked mode. If she was then this was worse than a Nosey. *She saw you and this is just pre-empting her giving you in. She wants you to see his widow.*

I waved her in, motioning her towards a tatty dining chair that occupied the room. She flicked her head around scanning the room, if I had known female company had been due then I may have spruced the old place up, maybe some flowers or something.

'Sit down,' I said. Once seated she sat with her longs legs crossed at an angle, 'So, what can I do for you?'

'It's more what you have done for us.' She could be his wife.

'Oh! And what would that be?' I paused and sat back and crossed my arms, using these gestures to bluff her with a façade of arrogance. No, not the wife. I couldn't image them hand in hand. The mother, she must be his mother, those long slender fingers guiding him in the ways of life.

'You took something of ours. Something very important.' What a strange way to talk about a person – *it*.

'Oh my!' I was now boarding on sarcasm.

'Yes', she gulped, tears surely not far off.

'That sounds very unpleasant. But I really don't know what.' I brushed the lint off my shoulder as if to demonstrate a hint of pride in these surroundings. 'As you can see, I am a man–' .

She cut me off massively. 'You did it.'

This sentence was a quick checkmate and I should have known it was coming. My body felt fidgety with a mixture of guilt and annoyance. Whilst assessing my next move I stared hard at this visitor. She had something on me and I didn't know what yet. Was she there? Had she been told?

'I'm awfully sorry but I don't know what you are on about'. I stared at her blankly.

'Come off, you know don't you?' This rhetorical question confirmed her power and control at this moment. I needed to know her evidence though, if it was hearsay then I could may be rebuff her, fob her off as mistaken. The need for me to know her hand shot up like mercury in a thermometer.

'I really don't understand what led you to me', I said itching for some unfounded information that I could debunk and which would hand the power and control of this conversation back to me.

'Look, be quiet and listen. You killed him with that van of yours. Then you left him for dead on a pavement.' She was getting frustrated here and her control was slipping.

I dug in.

'Whatever you are accusing me of you better have proof. You can't just waltz up to a gentleman's residence and lob accusations at him in the middle of the night. You need proof because otherwise there is nothing on me. So, tell me what you have got and we can do a little negotiation. Happy?' I immediately regretted using the word "negotiation".

'We saw you kill him.'

I grimaced, my face offended at this, such an ugly phrase. I was going to have to concede here, but not before I got these matters squared.

'Was he your husband?' I said looking to the floor.

'No' she snappily dismissed. 'He was not my husband'.

'Your son?'

'No, he was not my husband or son or lover or any other tag you want to join us with. He was a wanted criminal.'

I gulped and stared into her eyes.

'A criminal?'

'Yes, a criminal'.

'What had he done?'

'Nothing to concern you'

'Wait a minute, I may or may not have… a man who was a criminal? What's your interest in all of this?'

'Look, my role is not important. He was wanted back in my…'

The sudden feeling of having a Nosey sat right here in my abode, of having let a Nosey in ravaged me. Anger drew up into my torso and spread to my limbs. My mind shook with venom, how could I be so stupid?

'Are you one of them?' I snarled

'If you mean the law enforcement of your country, no. I enforce the law but… well… somewhere else. Look, what you did tonight we are very grateful for.'

Anger was replaced by a shaky, emptiness as my body shivered. 'Grateful?'

'Yes, grateful. I was supposed to kill him but fate stepped in and you did the dirty deed for me, so we want to give you a gift.'

She reached into the interior pocket of her coat. Her face contorted in the grimace of one who knows something is there but knows it is just out of reach.

'Ahh,' she said withdrawing an object, 'this is for you.'

I reached out and took it from her hand. She had given me 'a Polaroid-style photo with a half inch tear in the left hand corner, the edges were bent and creased. I looked at the back as if that held some interest too then reverted my gaze to the image.

'What's all this about?' I enquired as I took in this seemingly irreverent object. The photo was a black and white image of a two women. One was tall with curly hair and a stocky physique, the other smaller and freckled with hair tied back. They were no more than about ten years old. 'A photo of two kids?'

'I have carried this with me for most of my life. However, time is running out so I'm going to give it to you, *causa mortis.*'

'*Causa mortis?*' I pulled a face of confused lines.

'Yes, causa… never mind. It's yours now, so keep it safe. The image is quite old, so its accuracy it well, open but it is all we have. However, you must keep this safe. In the future one of these two visit you...'

'What the hell for?' I interjected.

'What you did tonight will put a price on your head, not in this world but… somewhere else… Anyway, you do need to know is that if they visit you must kill them'.

I shifted uncomfortably in my seat. All I wanted right now was to hand the photo back and tell this woman or whatever the hell she was to get the hell out of my flat. I hated her, largely because she was in control, she had the power. I wanted the power and I wanted the control but was never going to get it.

'You are asking me to kill…'

'They won't be kids when they come to see you' she said pre-empting any moral dilemma I was beginning to float. 'They will be adults and very dangerous adults. What you did tonight has major repercussions… but not for now. What I'm giving is a gift of life, because otherwise you will be dead.'

She rose and her hand headed to the door catch. 'Thank you and goodbye.'

Then she was gone and I was sat on my chair with a Polaroid of two kids in my left and an envelope of money in my right. I never saw her again. I never saw him in the news. The experience had unsettled me deeply, like stranger's fingers dipping into my brain. Whatever the hell they were it dynamited my self-confidence, there is nothing more unsettling than unseen hands twiddling and fiddling with your controls. The unknowing, I hate the unknowing because it means I'm ceding control and that doesn't sit well with me.

Despite all that I have kept that photo in my pocket all these years. Knowing that they would come.

Now, where is it? Oh, here it is. My eyesight isn't as good as it used to be. Things go a little blurry with time. Funny, how a photo freezes a moment in time. Now, if I hold it up to the light I can pick out little bits of this moment in time. A little dimple here, a little crease there. I've often been wondering what they grew up into, so just come a little closer.

CEZARIJA ABARTIS

Cezarija Abartis lives and works in St Cloud Minnesota USA where she teaches at the State University.

She has published a collection of short fiction, *Nice Girls and Other Stories* (New Rivers Press) and stories in *Baltimore Review, Bennington Review, FRiGG, matchbook, Waccamaw*, and *New York Tyrant*, among others. Her flash, "The Writer," was selected by Dan Chaon for Wigleaf's Top 50 online Fictions of 2012 and "To Kiss a Bear" was selected for Wigleaf's Longlist 2016.

Recently Cezarija completed writing a crime novel.

COMMENDED
OUEN PRESS
SHORT STORY COMPETITION 2019

COMMISERATION & GIFTS

by Cezarija Abartis

Mother Nature determined she would make creatures who never asked to live but with a life instinct that would not let them die. They would forever bumble about in pain, in optimism, believing that things (they, the situation, Life) would improve, and as dawn was about to break, she would pull the rug out from under them and chortle with wise joy, with see-I-told-you joy. She would fashion creatures who did not ask to be born, and then inflict misery upon them, and not allow them to cease until . . . until she grew bored and pointed a fiery finger at that dark woman on the hospital bed or that blond boy falling off a bicycle. And then she would start her amusement all over again with someone else. They would want to live forever and would despair because they could not. She would fool them, give them spurts of ebullience until she wore them out.

o0o

Paula had a cough. Not bad, just her typical March respiratory infection, called *ague* in the Renaissance. Despite her vitamins she still got viruses. Paula had written that meditation and ascribed it to Marcus Aurelius, then decided she needed an imaginary friend, Agnes Aurelius. Or maybe Tiffany Aurelius. Tiffany Alexa Aurelius, who always caught agues. Tiffany Agnes Aurelius, swell Roman-Pennsylvanian philosopher and community activist.

Hamlet and Macbeth gazed into the abyss and articulated their frightful despair; most people just mumbled and stumbled. *I have of late, but wherefore I know not, lost all my melancholy.* Paula laughed at her mangled pastiche. She was clever all right.

In the Music Department there was a suicide, Ben Becker, someone she knew slightly, an acquaintance, who smiled and joked, never seemed depressed. And she heard that Larry, decades ago her first love on the faraway west coast, had been diagnosed with oesophageal cancer and died only fifteen months later.

Well, he had fifteen months, but it must have been a series of doctors' appointments, tests, scans, hope, treatments, drugs, loss of hair, friends' visits and good-byes, hospital, hospice.

Ben Becker in Music, he was nothing like her mother. He was a devout Christian, an ex-alcoholic; he attended AA meetings; he laughed and told homely midwestern jokes when he played guitar at the local coffeehouse: *"Ole is so cheap that after his airplane landed safely, he grumbled to Lena: 'Vell, der goes five dollars down da drain for dat flight insurance!'"*

Paula put down her pen after grading a couple of

the freshman compositions about *The Yellow Wallpaper.*

Her own mother hadn't been a joker, but glum, methodical, and when she committed suicide, she drove to the bridge, stepped out of the car, and before anyone could stop her, jumped into the Ohio River. As far as anyone could tell, no particular event motivated her – not the loss of a job or child or spouse. No bad news from a doctor nor relative nor politician.

Outside Paula's office, the wind roared like trucks. She hoped the birds had a southern home. The weatherman said it was twenty-eight miles per hour; branches swayed; twigs clicked against the windows. Maybe they wanted to come in out of the bad weather.

She switched to reading students' journals on *All Quiet on the Western Front.*

"It's crazy that they don't have food."

"That stinks that he has to get boots from a dead man."

"What is a 'turnip'?"

"It's crazy that they have to put up barbed wire."

"It's crazy that the hospital won't give them morphine."

"It's crazy that they exchange cigarettes for bread."

Maybe they were right. Maybe it was crazy.

Her annual physical (now called Wellness Exam!) was scheduled for next week. Tomorrow they would draw blood, and she would fast tonight. No coffee in the morning. Drat.

Caroline called. "*Did they want to go to Ben's memorial service?*" "*It would be a nice gift to the family, a show of respect.*" Their friend Andrea was out of town, but she sent her thoughts and prayers. The three of them had gone to Ben's concerts. Had sat at the table in the coffee house sipping a glass of wine, tapping the rhythm on the tabletop, smiling at each other peacefully, enjoying his music.

You never really knew people. You thought you did, but they remained mysteries.

Caroline suggested a restaurant for dinner. *"I tried calling you at home. Then I figured you were on campus."* They would meet in half an hour.

Paula put her coat on, her boots, her gloves. When she went out on the sidewalk, the snow was in windrows, crisp-crunchy, the wind so forceful that her earlier footsteps were gone. At home, she would need to fill the birdfeeders, so that the sparrows, chickadees, nuthatches would not starve.

At a booth in the small Mexican restaurant, Caroline sat with a tissue to her nose. She sneezed. Tex-Mex music, cheery and insistent, flowed through the room. The neon beer signs winked invitingly above the counter, the strings of multicolored lights hanging from the ceiling twinkled, the ceiling fan moved the air so they would all stay protected and warm.

Paula dropped her coat on the bench. Caroline sighed and pulled a hand through her hair wearily. She must've been to the beauty salon – her hair was a shade redder. Paula did not believe in dye jobs for herself. Not honesty – just too much work to keep up the appearance of jollity and attentiveness.

'I like your hair.'

Caroline looked up. 'I'm sad about Ben.'

Paula settled into the booth. The restaurant was warm, smelled rich with spices. Outside the front window, the setting sun shone purple, crimson, and gold above the snow-covered roofs and parking lot.

'He was a good man.'

'Generous, funny, kind, sweet.'

Paula pulled out a napkin from the dispenser. 'Talented. Wonderful musician. He could've been a professional musician. He should've had a group. He was wonderful onstage. Great presence.'

'We were lovers once. A long time ago.'

Paula's breath folded in on itself. 'I didn't know. I'm sorry.'

'It didn't last.' Caroline's voice was soft but persistent. 'It was mutual. We decided to break up. And I met Eric. Ben didn't sour me on men.'

'You never mentioned him.'

'I was lonely in my job. I did tell Andrea. I didn't talk about it to anyone here. It was when she and I both happened to be interviewing for jobs in Atlanta. Neither of us got the jobs, of course.'

'She never told me.'

Did they keep other secrets from her? Was there a private club of people in the know?

'I asked her not to mention it to anyone. I didn't want it to get back to the people at work.'

'Yes, Andrea's discreet.' Paula shifted on the bench to avoid the setting sun streaming through the front window. She thought she was discreet herself, that Caroline could've told her.

A waiter came to take their orders. Caroline ordered her veggie burrito; she was a virtuous vegan; she never disapproved of meat eaters. Paula would have if she were a vegetarian. The waiter was a college-age kid, maybe someone Paula would see in her classes, brown hair, diamond or zircon earrings, tattoo of a mermaid on his right arm. She wondered about drowning women as a tattoo motif. She wondered if anybody loved Shakespeare enough to have his face tattooed on their body. He smiled in a goofy way. His aftershave was strong. What was his secret? Was he trying to be attractive? He left to bring them drinks.

Caroline's fingers walked on the table in front of the silverware. She had beautiful hands. She could've been a model for hand lotion with her iridescent skin and slim fingers. But she was an artist at an ad agency.

'I moved on. I fell in love with Eric. Ben went on to marry Belinda. They were perfect for each other.'

She made an X on the table with her forefinger.

'Eric and I were not perfect for each other.'

The waiter brought a beer for Caroline and poured coffee for Paula. His hand shook and he spilled coffee, which looked like a snaking river on the white Formica tabletop.

'Sorry.' He bent over and wiped up the river.

Paula looked over his shoulder and saw a pretty waitress watching him from the kitchen door. Her forehead was furrowed. The girl too was worried about something. Maybe she was flunking her college lit class or her restaurant management course. She tightened her blond hair in the ponytail. The waiter stumbled as he walked toward the kitchen. They all wore jeans and *Jolly Burrito* t-shirts showing a smiling burrito in a sombrero.

Paula sipped the coffee, wanting to enjoy it. She wouldn't be able to have it in the morning. 'Ben never seemed depressed to me.'

'That was when Ben worked in the music store, before it went out of business. He overworked. He didn't have time for depression, just furiously working. I called him a ball of fire. I drew pictures of him as a burning comet flaming toward Earth, a flashing blazing diamond, a burning bush, Moses encountering God. He laughed at me and said he was not good with bushes and gardens. I still have some of those drawings. He was a beautiful man.'

Her shoulders sagged and Paula could imagine Caroline as an old woman, with dyed red hair gray at the roots, and what flickered through her mind was a picture of herself as old too.

Another waiter, wiry and small, with frizzy hair and no tattoos, brought the food. 'Brian is on break,' he said. 'Enjoy.'

Brian stood outside the kitchen door talking to the waitress. He stepped toward her, brushed something off her shoulder. Was he flirting with her? Her arms were crossed, but she laughed at what he said. The setting sun lit up her hair in a blonde blaze.

Paula's phone buzzed. Her brother. His mother-in-law's diagnosis had come in: Dementia with Lewy Bodies. He needed to go and comfort his wife. Paula explained to Caroline. 'It's like Alzheimer's and Parkinson's, and the late stage could involve paranoia and hallucinations and inability to move. You just sit there in terror, with horrible ghosts whispering over your shoulder.'

Caroline shuddered. 'Worse than what's facing me.'

She linked and unlinked her hands. She should've had a husband to kiss her hands every day.

'I'm trying to decide whether to leave Eric or not. Or maybe he'll leave me.' She erupted into a laugh, but it was abrupt, tinny. 'He's seeing someone else. We clawed our way to this, to each other, and look what happens. We let go. Or it drifted away. Eric and I, it was so hard to get together. And now . . .' She brushed taco chip crumbs off the edge of the table.

Paula imagined the crumbs falling over a cliff, yelling all the way down. They screamed *Help!* as they scattered, their little crumb-arms pinwheeling. Caroline's sweater was the color of golden cake crumbs. They splashed as they hit water at the bottom and sank.

'Who is the other woman?'

'Someone from work. Amy. One of the new lawyers.' Caroline twirled her fork in her beans and rice. 'Do you like living alone?' she put down her fork. 'Is it okay?'

Paula sat back. 'I have friends.'

Her voice felt little.

'Yes, but don't you want somebody with you?' Caroline brushed her fingers clean. 'That sounds insulting. I don't mean to suggest that you're so feeble that you need someone.'

'But it's true, I do feel feeble,' she put her hands in her lap, as if to keep them from falling. 'But there it is. That's life.' She stopped pressing the crumbs on the floor with her foot. 'I can't get a better job. My colleagues are dopey. The economy is failing. Climate change is happening. Species of insects and mammals are dying out. My mother committed suicide. I want to make a safe nest and can't. Our species is only sixty thousand years old. The dinosaurs had a hundred million years.' Her voice was getting shrill.

'Almost one hundred eighty million years,' Caroline looked toward the window, 'but they still exist in the birds.' A gray bird flitted around a snow-covered branch of the tree at the edge of the parking lot. 'I suppose that's some consolation.'

To be out of all this struggle. Paula's mother had said that. 'What am I going to do? Just complain about my students? Tiffany doesn't write the journals, misses class because her car breaks down, doesn't do the oral presentation, emails that she has the flu. Marcus says he's lost interest in the course. Alexa sits in class memorising definitions from her flash cards for her Psych major. James has a retinal detachment in his left eye and will have a hard time reading for a few weeks. Geez.' Was she becoming a crazy lady? The marimbas became loud and hectic. 'And I can't find my notes on Hamlet.'

Caroline reached for her hand. 'It will be all right.'

'No, it won't. Suicide rates are rising. And I'm exhausted.' Paula coughed. It flared up and down her oesophagus and stopped. She wanted to escape from the nest of sticky reeds and mucus-mud.

Caroline patted her hand and withdrew it. 'You need to rest and relax.' Caroline let out a small cough too, pulled out a tissue and blew her nose. 'I'm sorry I asked to meet.'

'I need to be out of this striving,' Paula blinked.

Across the table, Caroline looked worn and watery.

'My problems are small compared to yours. I mean, I can't find my notebook. But you, you're losing your husband.'

Caroline snorted, 'Now I do sound pathetic.' She folded over a corner of her napkin and tore a neat line and then another. 'It's true. I am a loser.'

'I didn't mean that. Not at all.'

'Now I'm making you feel bad.' Caroline tore another line in the napkin.

'I should open up a shoe store. My foot is always in my mouth.'

She shook her head. 'I don't even know what that means. We'll be okay. Your notebook will turn up.' Caroline stretched out her napkin on the table, pressed it with her fingers as if she could restore the tears. 'At least I didn't die in a plane crash or Ebola outbreak or hurricane flooding.' Her mouth was wide in a smile but pained.

'That's not funny. I dreamed that my kitty had fallen in the river, and I jumped in after her and began sinking. She picked me up by the scruff of my neck and carried me to the river bank. Happy ending.' She opened her hands theatrically, as if for applause.

'I had a dream like that where I slid down the sloppy river bank. All around me sailboats, in the distance were church towers, and nearby a bridge. No cats.'

'Not happy.'

'It felt like falling asleep. No thrashing, no pain. Just a soft drift to the abyss. Not painful, not thorny. More like warm sinking.'

'Half in love with easeful death?'

'What?'

'You remember. Keats.'

'Oh, right. Keats. Who died of tuberculosis, lungs drowning in blood.'

'We have treatments for tuberculosis now.'

'Right. If only he had lived another two hundred years.'

'Or been born now.'

'If he lived now, would he have been a poet? Or would he have designed video games?'

'Nothing wrong with that,' Caroline shrugged. 'My agency has a couple clients.'

'And that's what my students want to do. Or play during class. I'm told that years ago they used to read newspapers, in the back of the room.' She glanced around the tables, at the twenty-year-olds laughing with each other, lifting their beers. 'My students could be my cat to whom I'm reading Hamlet. They're not evil but they don't really care.' She stabbed at her burrito. 'Well, it beats digging ditch, as one of my retired colleagues said.'

'My clients want memorable ad campaigns.' Caroline pulled out a tissue and blew her nose. 'I'm playing Beethoven for the dogs.' Caroline put away her tissue. 'They like the high notes, I'm told.'

'I should just learn to enjoy that.'

Out of the corner of her eye, she watched their waiter with the strong aftershave. She had forgotten his name. Brian? Bruce? He leaned in to the next table and seemed to waiver as if there were a wind indoors. He smiled to the two middle-aged couples eating their burritos.

She heard him say, 'I proposed marriage to my girlfriend.' He proudly nodded toward the pretty waitress who was serving a table by the door. 'She agreed, but first I have to quit smoking.'

The two plump couples at the table glanced toward the waitress and smiled knowingly, approvingly.

Paula wondered if the girlfriend had asthma or control issues or was genuinely concerned about his health. Or didn't want to be a widow. Or all of the above. When Paula was in love with Ken, she didn't care that he smoked, though she did care that he still had phone conversations with his ex-wife and laughed. Paula had not thought she was jealous. She later forgave him. She didn't forgive herself for a long time. She should have made it work. Jealousy was not even one of the seven deadly sins. The closest candidate was covetousness.

Well, at least she didn't smoke. At least she had health insurance. At least teaching beat digging ditch. She agreed. It was better than working in the coal mines or the polluted cities of China and Africa. She felt ashamed for indulging her malaise. She had no right to feel sorry for herself in this world of misery and poverty. She was lucky: let her dance for joy! Let her cavort and career and jump but not off a bridge.

She had too much time, too much wealth. The luxury of existential melancholy.

The waiter, carrying a tray of coffees and desserts, glanced at their table, moved on, bumped his shoulders to the music of Flaco Jimenez. The tune was vigorous and joyful. It put to the side the hard lives and bruises of the peasants and waltzed with its implausible, perfect mix of accordions and guitars. On the wall, a new poster of women wearing flounced dresses and high combs in their dark hair, castanets on their fingers. They danced off the wall. The waiter, in the middle of the room, tripped against a table of young men loudly celebrating a birthday. He fell. The tray crashed. The blonde waitress ran to him where he sat on the floor. He raised one hand up in victory and said, 'I'm okay.' Did he mean it, or was he merely reassuring all of them as he smiled painfully?

The waitress explained to the room, 'Somebody falls every week and doesn't get hurt.' She reached out a hand to help up the fallen waiter.

'That was exciting,' Caroline said, watching him limp to the kitchen. 'Poor guy. I hope he wasn't hurt. I hope he doesn't have to pay for the broken dishes.'

'Do you think he was drunk?'

'This early in the day?'

'I smelled strong aftershave or mouthwash. Menthol, peppermint, something intense.'

'I have a cold.'

The blonde waitress came by to clear their dishes. 'I hope he's all right,' Caroline said.

'He has a trick ankle.' The waitress took in a deep breath and looked away. 'From a sports injury.' She smiled widely, bravely. She had delicate fingers ending in glittery nails. Paula supposed the waitress was in Elementary Education or maybe Marketing. She didn't really know that. She thought the waiter was drunk. She was being condescending and judgmental.

'I'm going to the bathroom,' Caroline said.

She walked across the room, carefully stepping around the broken crockery on the wet floor. She, too, looked tired.

As a child Paula had wanted to escape her parents, childhood, class. In her group years ago, she was the newest arrival, the newest pursuer of the American Dream. She ran to study Shakespeare, away from her class, her blue-collar group, especially her mother. She and her mother were both hard workers. Her grandparents had been in a refugee camp and been sponsored by a friend to come to the U.S. Yay! Her grandparents had the heart of their lives cut out, but now it was replaced. Yay! Yippee! On Sundays, when her mother didn't work in the factory, she took Paula and her brother to matinees of cowboy movies with the hero in the white hat overcoming the villain. That was the right thing.

The waiter wanted to get married. Her brother had said that when their first child was born he dreamed that he was in a motorboat and he pressed the gas pedal to speed away. He turned to see little Lawrence in a dinghy tied to his boat by a thick rope, and he was wailing.

The short waiter brought the bill and shook his head. 'He's drunk again. He's going to lose his job. He's a loser. I got him this job. For Darla. She's my sister.' He held his notepad professionally. He could've been a journalist witnessing an execution. He went to the cash register.

So: she had been right about the tall waiter, not that it concerned her. The sun had set, but there was alternate and welcome light because of the gleaming snow. The waitress piled the dishes, turned toward the window. 'After work we're going to look at the iced-over river. They're saying it's finally frozen over and beautiful with the clean snow falling on it.'

'Is your friend okay?'

Her eyes slid to the side. 'Yes, he'll be okay.'

Paula wondered if this was the complete truth. Darla picked up the silverware.

Caroline came back and sat in the booth. She smiled at the waitress. 'Are you in school here?'

'I'm a physics major.' The waitress nodded shyly. 'I want to go on to get a degree in astrophysics. I love math and nature and the stars,' she shrugged. 'It's a long haul, I realise. Who knows why you love things?'

She peered over her shoulder at the waiter. He was

gesturing widely with his hands to the manager, a tall man with a severe expression on his face. The waiter's hands were perfect hands: large, flat, accommodating. They did not seem the hands of a drunk.

'It's a beautiful planet,' the waitress said. 'Four-point-five billion years in a universe of thirteen-point-eight billion.' She raised her chin at the table of young men in the middle of the room celebrating. The guys raised their been steins and toasted the guy at the end. She let out a laugh. The accordions stretched out the notes. The beer sign blinked yellow and gilded the people sitting at the counter. Everyone looked warm and golden while the snow seemed blue outside. She clapped. 'We should hold a birthday party for the planet.'

Paula was not able to impose Happy Birthday on the music, maybe because it was dance-y and exuberant. The music evened out, softened, and died down. A new song came up on the music service, also regular, loud, and happy.

At home her cat would greet her at the door. He would meow at her and lead her to the food bowl. She was becoming an old lady caring for an old cat. Well, so be it. She should think of the beauty of the crystal-covered twigs and branches, magical transformations into picture postcards, the fluffy, vague, unshaped snow like round dinosaurs, the boulevards pillowed with gleam, feathered with promise. These were gifts too.

'I gotta go,' Caroline said, her hand on her coat. 'I need to work on some story boards.'

They left a large tip for the servers.

OTHER PUBLICATIONS
FROM OUEN PRESS

Biography...

THE SOHO DON
by Michael Connor is a biographical narrative about a London gangster whose unique power was strongest in the 25 years after World War II - a very powerful read. The Krays said he feared no-one, and was the one man they truly respected. Likened to Graham Greene's period thriller *Brighton Rock*, and the style of Truman Capote's *In Cold Blood.*

KNIGHT: Yorkshireman, Storyteller, Spy
by Greg Christie is an epic tale of an extraordinary man who reinvented himself as artist, soldier, newspaper reporter, film critic, intelligence officer. A major inter-war novelist whose work was lauded by the literary establishment of the 1930s – but overshadowed by his biggest hit – a little pot-boiler he sold for $10,000 he called *Lassie Come-Home.*

Crime thrillers...

IMAGINE GHOSTS TELLING TALES IN FRONT OF SMOKY MIRRORS
by S.L.Masunda – is a fictional memoir exploring a writer's quest for literary recognition. The atrocities he commits in the name of ambition become increasingly gruesome, but we are drawn back in time to reveal pivotal moments in the writer's life that challenge the reader to seek out redemption for our hero turned killer.

MAY ALL YOUR NAMES BE FORGOTTEN
by Michael Connor – a fast moving crime thriller set in south London, containing as many pointers for budding telesales staff, prepared to break the rules, as it does for the ordinary citizen seeking to avoid being hustled.

THE UNCOMMON PRISON OF HENRY V HENRY ***by Simon Bullivant*** – The gruesome murder of a young girl hits the headlines. A compulsive hoarder of hard-copy news, finds his interest in the crime becomes obsessive. The Police have their own suspicions, which include placing him ever closer to the crimes. A compelling story of a man's transformation from a marginalised, invisible human being, who inhabits a world of his own creation, into an individual who finds the means to escape.

Rites of passage...

THE MUSHROOM EFFECT ***by Michael Connor*** – **A powerful portrayal of egos, betrayal, torment, resilience & resolution.** Erminia, a talented chef climbing the celebrity ladder, opens her first restaurant – foraging for 'Wild Food' plays a big part in her recipe creations and leads her to an amazing culinary discovery. But, pride and ambition cloud her judgement It's a painful journey for Erminia's suffering mind as she attempts to come to terms with the failure of everything she has thought to be true, or considered to be of value.

CODY, THE MEDICINE MAN AND ME
by Alan Wilkinson – a trip across the USA transforms into the ultimate voyage of personal discovery. Attempting to establish the truth of his baffling ancestry, Ray West struggles to prepare himself for a reunion with his estranged twin brother – old rivalries quickly resurface. **A showdown brews – but ultimately only one of the brothers can ride off into the sunset.**

THE CLEANSING ***by Michael Connor*** – weaves a powerful plot, full of vivid encounters and fascinating characters. It depicts the harsh reality that still faces many, particularly the women, in Africa today.

Other short story collections...

LAST CALL & OTHER SHORT STORIES ***including Ouen Press Short Story Competition Winners 2015*** – a variety of fictitious working-dogs portrayed in many different circumstances as their 'jobs' dictate or their conditions demand; a collection of compelling tales that reflect that vast, often unfathomable melting-pot of human emotions and intention.

JOURNEY THROUGH UNCERTAINTY & OTHER SHORT STORIES ***including Ouen Press Short Story Competition Winners 2016*** – featuring physical and emotional journeys, endured and enjoyed, with humour and courage – each one a testimony to a place, or an event, or a sentiment.

TASTING NOTES & OTHER SHORT STORIES ***including Ouen Press Short Story Competition Winners 2017*** – a complex and diverse menus of science fiction, art, humour, the spying game, magical realism, celebrity cooking and much more, expertly crafted to tantalise and entertain.